covet

MICALEA SMELTZER

On the run from the Iniquitous, Mara feels lost and helpless. Without Theo by her side she's left bare and vulnerable, but she's a fighter and, with blood boiling in her veins, she vows to avenge him.

The Iniquitous have already taken so much from her, and she refuses to sit back and let them take anything else. She trains harder, preparing herself physically and mentally to take them on. As her magic grows stronger, so does the voice speaking to her from beyond the grave.

She wants to believe it's real, to give in to what feels *right*, but if she does, her mind might be lost forever.

chapter one

THE TREES AND ENDLESS ROADS bled around us.

I was naïve to think things could be good.

I got comfortable.

I got *happy*.

And it was all ripped right out from under me.

Destruction followed me wherever I went. It was like I was a magnet. Anger bubbled and festered inside me like a living thing. I felt suffocated by it, but I was either too strong, or too stubborn, to die.

"Mara," Adelaide whispered beside me, breaking the silence that had descended on the car in the last five hours since we fled the mansion.

I slowly turned my head to look at her. Mascara was dried on her cheeks, and her eyes were red-rimmed.

The loss of Theo made me feel like half of myself had been ripped savagely out of my body. I no longer felt whole. But I knew his loss was equally as difficult for her. He was her brother, her only family she had left.

"What?" I whispered. My voice was hoarse and raw. I hadn't spoken since I stopped screaming out the window for Theo.

"We shouldn't be sad," her voice cracked. "He was doing his job, his duty, what he was born to do. We should be proud."

I looked away from her and back out the window beside me, afraid I'd begin to cry again. I didn't want to cry anymore. I didn't want to be weak. I had to be strong. Without Theo, I had to stay alert and protect myself. In the window, my reflection stared back at me, my eyes vacant, my freckles stark against my pale skin. I looked like a ghost. It was how I felt, too. A shell of the girl I'd been only a few hours before, declaring her love to her soul mate.

I knew he was doing his duty, but it didn't make it any easier.

In fact, it made it a little worse.

If he didn't have to protect me he wouldn't have been there. He would've fled with us.

Actually, none of this would've probably happened in the first place.

I felt eyes on me, and when I turned slightly my eyes collided with Ethan's in the rearview mirror. When they met, he quickly looked back at the road.

I had no idea where we were going to go or what we were going to do.

In the big scheme of things we were *kids* and ill-prepared for this.

Victor's last words echoed in my mind.

"G-Get away f-from here. F-Find C-Cleo. She h-holds the k-key."

Who was this Cleo? I'd never heard the name before and had no idea how I was supposed to find this person. Maybe it wasn't even a person. It could have been a place for all I knew.

"Is anybody hungry?" Ethan asked.

"Yes," Winston and Adelaide answered while I gave a mumbled no.

It was light out now, which meant it was safe for us to stop, but I wanted to keep going.

And going.

And *going*.

There was a part of me that thought I could escape my racing thoughts, stop replaying Theo's last moments over and over again, but my logical self knew it was impossible.

Ethan pulled into a café and parked. I didn't even know what state we were in—if we were still in Washington or had crossed a line somewhere along the way. "We'll grab food and eat as we go. You guys go get some things and I'll get gas." He pointed across the road to a station.

"You want anything?" Adelaide asked him.

"I'm not picky. Get me whatever."

He reached over in front of Winston and pulled down the glove box. He found a bundle of cash and handed Winston some to cover our food. There must've been several thousand dollars in the stack and for all I knew more was hidden in the car.

Even though I didn't want to get out, I did, and followed the others inside.

The café was small, with only room for two small tables and chairs and the counter where you ordered. The walls were painted a bright green with flowers stenciled on them. I couldn't help but be reminded of the home I grew up in and the fruit stenciled on the kitchen walls. My dad said my mother did it, but now I wasn't so sure.

So much I believed to be true was a lie.

I didn't feel like I could even trust my own memories and it sucked majorly.

Winston ordered first, then Adelaide for her and Ethan, and then it was my turn.

I ordered a breakfast sandwich, even though I doubted I could eat, and a coffee.

The three of us waited off to the side for our order to be ready. The patrons eyed us with curiosity. I'm sure we looked strange, me in my fighting clothes and the two of them dressed up from the Christmas Eve ball.

I felt Winston and Adelaide watching me, studying me, wondering if I was okay or might run off at any second.

I *wanted* to run, but I couldn't.

Not when Theo sacrificed his life for mine.

I was still alive and, while I was, it was my duty to kill every last one of the Iniquitous.

They killed my mom, they killed my dad, they even killed Ian, and now they'd taken Theo from me too.

I wouldn't stand for that.

I wanted them to suffer as much as me.

My mind played out creative scenarios of how I'd kill them.

A knife to the eye, choking until I saw the life leave them, lighting them on fire with my magic—I'd burn the whole world down if that's what it took to kill them all.

"Order number two," the lady called out.

Winston grabbed the bag of food while Adelaide grabbed the drink carrier, which left me with nothing, so I grabbed a handful of napkins to feel semi-useful.

Ethan was parked back out front and we all piled inside.

It took a minute to pass the food and drinks around, but once they were, Ethan was back on the road and we were putting even more miles between us and the manor.

I felt sick Theo was left there, or worse, the Iniquitous had taken his body with them.

I'd barely had time to revel in what transpired between us before all hell broke loose.

But those stolen moments with him, I knew I'd cherish them forever. They'd been some of the best and happiest times of my life. I never knew I could love someone so much and be loved in return. It was the stuff love songs and stories were written about. Even if he was gone, our love wasn't. A love like that didn't go away because he was gone. If anything, it grew stronger. Besides, it was better to have loved and lost someone as great as Theo than to have not tried at all. The odds were against us from the start, we weren't supposed to be together for reasons I still didn't know, but for one night I'd known what it'd be like for us to love each other openly.

It was everything.

I nibbled on my sandwich, barely tasting it.

I noticed Adelaide picked at hers too. Nigel eyed me angrily and I couldn't tell whether he was hungry or being a cat.

When I'd hardly eaten a quarter of my sandwich, I wrapped it up and put it back in the bag. My stomach was rolling, and I knew I'd get sick if I forced myself to eat any more.

Adelaide frowned at me, like she was saddened by my lack of effort, but then she sighed and stuffed the rest of her sandwich in the bag.

Theo had died only *hours* ago. There was no way I could function like a normal human being yet. I was still processing, and I feared I might never be normal again.

Yeah, he was an arrogant asshole, but he was *my* arrogant asshole.

He was as much as extension to me as my hands. I felt lost without him and I didn't know how I'd made it nearly eighteen years without him. As my protector, he and I were connected on a level that was special and unique, I trusted him more than I did anybody else without even being able to explain why. I just did.

I picked up my coffee and sipped at it slowly. It wasn't bad but it wasn't the best either. It helped settle my stomach, though, so at least there was that.

"Where are we going to go?" Adelaide asked hesitantly, her voice shaky. "This is *two* safe houses attacked now. Where will we be safe?"

Her question was valid and one I hadn't asked myself yet even though I should've. All I could think about was Theo being gone, when I should've been thinking about what came next.

Ethan sighed and tightened his hand around the steering wheel. "I don't know. I don't know," he repeated. I noticed how stressed and strained he looked.

"We can't keep driving," Winston interjected. "You need to sleep, man."

"We need to put as much distance between us and *them* as we can."

I leaned up between the two seats. "I can drive if you need to rest."

He shook his head adamantly. "Theo would kill me if I let you drive."

"Theo's not here to reprimand you. Adelaide can't drive—you can't, can you?" I glanced at her and she shook her head. "And Winston?" I probed.

"Only on the other side of the road, love. Never learned here."

"I'm your only option." I patted Ethan on the shoulder and he groaned.

"Fine, but I can go a little longer. Try and get some rest and we'll switch."

I nodded and sat back.

I doubted I could sleep, but I'd try.

Setting the coffee in the cup holder, I laid my head against the window.

I wiggled around and tried to get comfortable.

To my surprise, I drifted off to sleep within minutes.

***

The hall was long, endless, and no matter how fast I ran, the distance didn't seem to shorten.

"Run, Mara, run!" a voice called out, panicked and begging.

I looked back, searching for the voice, my heart breaking in two. All I saw behind me were the darkened figures chasing me. So many.

So. Freaking. Many.

I burst through a door into the open air, the sudden brightness blinding my eyes.

Something slammed into me from behind, and I screamed, kicking out.

"You're mine."

I stared into the face of my father. He glowered at me, his eyes lethal and feral.

"You can't escape me, little one."

"Mara!"

"Kill him," my father said over his shoulder. "Kill them all."

"Over my dead body," I shouted, before a light burst out of me and pushed him off.

His body flew through the air, back through the doorway, before hitting a wall and falling to the ground.

He wasn't dead.

Not yet.

But he would be.

I jolted awake, my body clammy with sweat, my heart racing, and my breaths ragged.

I pushed my hair out of my eyes, sick to my stomach from the dream.

Nightmare.

Vision.

Whatever it was.

"You okay, love?" Winston looked back at me. "You don't look well."

"I-I'm fine," I stuttered, trying to wrap my brain around what I saw.

It was the same dream I had before my graduation, only this time it was longer, more vivid.

More *real*.

"You sure?" He sounded doubtful.

"Yeah," I assured him with a wave of my hand.

Beside me, Adelaide was sound asleep with Nigel curled up in her lap.

"You ready to switch?" I asked Ethan.

"Soon," he replied. "We'll need gas again soon, so I'll stop then."

"How long have I been out?"

"Almost five hours," Winston told me.

"Did you sleep?" I asked him.

"Nah, I stayed awake to help Ethan. I'll switch spots with Adelaide when we stop and she can help keep you awake."

I didn't tell him, but I would've rather had silence than to have Adelaide trying to make forced conversation with me.

I didn't want to talk right now. All I could think about was Theo.

Those last moments.

The sword plunged through his body.

I held my breath and fought back tears before I grabbed the little jar attached to the necklace. The firefly fluttered madly against my hand. It provided a much-needed connection to Theo I desperately needed.

My body ached for him, like he was something vital I needed to live.

As important as food or water.

I let the necklace go and rifled through my backpack, searching through the things I'd packed months before. Theo hadn't been crazy when he told me I needed to be prepared.

Giving him credit wasn't something I liked to do, but he was usually right.

Closing it back up, I leaned back in my seat, closing my eyes.

I missed him. God, did I miss him.

It didn't seem possible to miss someone *this* much when you'd only seen them hours prior, but when faced with the reality I'd never see him again it *hurt* in unimaginable ways.

He understood me in ways nobody else did—in ways that didn't even need to be spoken.

I conjured his face in my mind, the floppy black hair, his perpetual scowl, the lip ring, and his narrowed gray eyes.

A tear leaked out of the corner of my eye.

He shouldn't be gone. It wasn't right, and I'd have to live with seeing his death.

It would never leave me, I knew.

I tamped down my emotions, refusing to give rise to the flood that threatened to overwhelm me. My strength was the only thing I could rely on now. I needed to keep my head above water so I could think and learn to avenge his death. His death would not be in vain. I wouldn't allow it.

I was born a Chosen One, for a *purpose*, and this was mine.

chapter two

I GRIPPED THE STEERING WHEEL SO tight I was surprised it didn't rip into two.

"You won't even look at me," Adelaide whispered beside me, and I cringed.

"I can look at you." I stole a quick glance before returning my eyes to the road.

Ethan had told me to drive, with no particular destination in mind, so that's what I was doing. We'd crossed into Nevada not too long ago.

"I'm your friend," she whispered softly. "You can talk to me."

I clenched my teeth. "No, I can't."

"Mara," she squeaked. "Don't shut me out. He's my brother."

"Was," I corrected.

"Stop it," she snapped.

"What?" I shot back. "It's the truth."

"I didn't know you could be so cruel." She crossed her arms over her chest and looked out the side window.

I sighed, feeling like shit for her hurting her. Adelaide had been a good friend to me from the moment I met her, and just because I was heartbroken didn't give me the right to lash out at her. It was easier to be mean, though. It eased the burn of the pain radiating in my chest, but I knew it was only a temporary fix—a pathetic Band-Aid that would rip off at a moment's notice.

"I'm sorry."

She snorted like my apology was pathetic. I guess it was.

"I loved him," I confessed. "Love," I corrected. Adelaide was right, it wasn't right to talk about him in the past tense. Not yet, at least. I did still love him, that wasn't something that was going to go away simply because he was gone.

"I know." Those two words held so much weight. Adelaide had known before we did that we were meant to be.

"I feel guilty."

"Why?" She looked at me. "You knew as well as I did the risks that come with him being your protector."

"Yeah, you might know the risks, but that doesn't make an outcome like this any easier to understand. We might be enchanters but we're still inherently human. We believe in *good*."

"You made him happier than anything or anyone ever has," she whispered, glancing in the back at the sleeping figures.

"I hope I did, at least a little; he was still a grumpy ass most of the time."

She laughed, the sound almost startling with the conversation. "Trust me, that was Theodore in a good mood."

"How are we going to prepare ourselves?" I asked her, glancing over my shoulder to change lanes. "You know they're going to try to find me."

Adelaide bit her lip. "Ethan's with us. He can teach us more about fighting and magic. Winston too."

"We have to hunt them first," I whispered to her.

"Mara ..." She paused, gathering her thoughts. "Do you think that's a good idea?"

"I refuse to be a sitting duck," I snapped. "I won't sit around and wait for them to find me. I'll find them on my own if I have to."

And I would. I'd leave them behind and find the Iniquitous on my own and kill as many of them as I could before I died. I wasn't going to sit on the bench, I was going to get out and play the game.

She stuttered a breath. "I'm in."

"What?" I snapped my head to her.

"I'm in," she repeated. "They *murdered* my brother. I won't let you take them down alone and get all the glory," she joked. "I want to have some fun too."

"I'm in too," Winston spoke sleepily.

"Me too," Ethan piped in.

I glanced in the rearview mirror at the two guys. "You don't think I'm crazy?"

"Well, I think you have to be a little nuts to take on the Iniquitous, but sometimes you have to take action. If everybody always sat back and did nothing, the world would crumble to pieces. You need the few who stand up and try to make a difference to see any change. I think enchanters have been hanging back too long, thinking the problem will solve itself, when it obviously won't. It's time to fight to reclaim our world again." Ethan spoke passionately, like this was something he'd been thinking about for a long time. "There are those, of course, who've always been quietly fighting but there's not enough of them. We need more. There's power in numbers."

"I'm tired of being scared," Winston confessed. "I don't want to spend my whole life looking over my shoulder." He snorted. "What am I saying, that's not a life, that's a prison."

It seemed impossible the four of us could make any kind of difference, but vengeance was a strong motivator.

"The older enchanters are scared," Ethan added. "Scared of dying. Scared of living. Scared of everything, honestly. But dying isn't scary, death is easy. I feel more fear at the thought of not trying. I'd rather try and fail, than to not try at all."

"Do ..." I paused, unsure if I should continue, but decided I might as well. "Do you know a Cleo?"

I couldn't erase Victor's last words from my mind. I knew they were important, but I didn't understand *how*.

"No," Ethan spoke. "I'm not familiar with the name. You?"

"Nah, sorry I'm not," Winston added.

Adelaide shrugged. "Me either."

"It must be important," I whispered, more to myself than them.

Victor wouldn't have spoken those words if they weren't. Somehow, I had to figure out what they meant.

"Go back to sleep," I told Ethan. "You need your rest."

He chuckled and I saw him salute me in the rearview mirror. "Yes, boss."

Both guys eventually drifted off to sleep and it was only Adelaide and me again.

"You guys looked happy," she murmured quietly.

"What?" I asked, confused.

"At the dance," she clarified. "You guys didn't notice me but I was watching."

I swallowed thickly. "It was the best night of my life," I replied honestly.

A night I'd cherish forever.

Theo had been the dusk to my dawn, and when we finally came together it was more unbelievable than I'd imagined. We were opposites in so many ways, but somehow the same at our core.

He was mine, and I was his, and even death wouldn't take that from us.

"I hope one day I find someone to love, like you guys love each other. You fought it for months, but even then it was obvious. It was the strongest kind of magic I've ever seen," she mused. "It was beautiful."

I swallowed thickly. "What am I going to do without him?"

She shrugged. "The best thing you can do is *live*. He died to give you the chance to live, so that's what you do."

I knew she was right, but it seemed impossible.

At the moment, I couldn't imagine ever feeling whole again.

I was a ghost, floating along aimlessly, lost without my tether to the real world.

"I want them to *die* for this," I growled out. "To suffer."

"They will," she promised.

She reached over then and turned up the radio. She must've sensed I didn't want to talk anymore and, for that, I was thankful.

I tried to empty my thoughts and drive, but it was hard.

It hadn't even been a whole day yet.

And beneath my sadness and anger there was fear.

They'd found me there, they wanted me, and they wouldn't rest until they got me.

I had to be stronger. Faster. Unstoppable.

***

It was dark out when we stopped for a second time and grabbed dinner. Again, we got something to eat in the car and gas. None of us felt safe yet to stay put for long.

We still didn't know where we were going, and it was probably best.

Ethan switched to driving and Adelaide and I piled in the back once more.

I didn't have an appetite but I knew if I wanted to keep my strength I'd have to eat. The pizzas we'd picked up weren't exactly healthy but beggars couldn't be choosers. I handed a slice to Ethan as he pulled out of the parking lot and another to Winston before taking one for myself.

We'd crossed up into Idaho before we switched driving and now Ethan was heading south into Utah. We were making a sort of zig-zag pattern. So far, from what we could tell, we hadn't been followed.

Which was good, I guess.

I didn't think the four of us were prepared to take them on.

We barely made it out from the manor as it was, and only because of Theo's sacrifice.

I finished my piece and grabbed another. I didn't think I could eat, but having had so little during the day, my body needed it. Adelaide was already on her third slice, so she must've felt the same.

"When do you think we can stop and get some real rest?" Winston asked Ethan.

Ethan shrugged, merging onto the highway. "Soon, I hope. I don't really want to stop at a hotel."

Winston sighed. "We can't run forever. What are we going to do?"

Ethan rubbed his jaw. He looked exhausted and worried. It was like he'd aged ten years in the last twenty-four hours. I'm sure since Theo had asked for his help he felt responsible for the three of us now, and with mine and Winston's status as Chosen Ones, the weight on his shoulders had to be unbearable. He probably didn't know about Winston, unless Theo told him, but still.

"I don't know," he admitted. "Right now, we need to find shelter. That's my top priority."

"How are we going to do that?" Adelaide asked. "I don't think any of the temporary safe houses are *safe*. If the Iniquitous know about the big ones, they'll know about those too."

"I know a place," Ethan admitted with a slight hesitation. "An old buddy of mine I knew from after I left Eldson Manor. I stayed with him a bit, and he's super paranoid about staying under the radar, so it's the safest place I can think of."

"Can he be trusted?" I asked. I hated to point it out, but it had to be said. The truth was, even if you thought you could trust someone, you really *couldn't*.

Someone leaked the locations of *two* safe houses, and somehow got the Iniquitous into Eldson manor during the masked ball.

My money was on Finn.

He was slimy.

Ethan sighed from the front seat. "Yeah, I'd trust him with my life. He's ... different, though."

"Different?" I repeated. "Different, how?"

"You know how Chosen Ones are *rare*?"

"Um ... yeah," I hesitated and Winston looked at him quizzically.

"There are others, more rare, believed to only be legend."

"And you're saying this guy is one of them?"

"He ..." He hesitated, tapping his thumbs against the steering wheel. "He knows things."

"Like he can see the future?" I asked.

"No, not quite. He gets a feel for things and he's always right. He's called a Window, because he can see through things."

"Did you know about this?" I asked Adelaide.

She shook her head. "Not at all."

"You learn something new every day," Winston added.

"His place is probably the safest for us. It's reinforced and few know about it. Just him and ... me."

"Interesting," I spoke softly, piecing things together.

"You can't tell anyone." Ethan glanced in the mirror.

I mimed zipping my lips. "You know we won't tell anyone about him."

He breathed a sigh of relief. "I would never forgive myself he was hurt because of me. I ..."

"You love him," I finished for him.

He nodded.

I would've never guessed Ethan was gay, but it didn't really matter. He was free to love who he wanted. I trusted Ethan and if he felt this guy was worthy of loving then I had to believe he'd be willing to shelter us and not give us up.

"What's his name?" I asked.

"Jee," he replied.

"That's a cool name."

He smiled and there was a slight twinkle in his eye like he was recollecting a fond memory. "He's Korean-American."

"How'd you meet?" I asked.

He chuckled. "That's enough questions, Mara. Get some sleep."

chapter three

ONCE WE DECIDED TO HEAD to Jee's it only took two days with stops.

Jee's place was located in downtown Minneapolis. I wasn't sure if the city was the safest place for us to be, but if Ethan thought this was best I was going to trust him.

For now.

The sky was dark when Ethan pulled into an underground garage and drove around stopping in front of a solid cinderblock wall.

I didn't even bother to question why. I wasn't surprised by anything anymore.

Ethan whispered something under his breath I couldn't make out. It sounded like a different language, one I'd never heard.

The wall shimmered like it was speckled in glitter. It still looked solid, but there the slightest glimmer proving it wasn't.

Ethan drove through it, and I held my breath.

I *knew* we'd get through fine, but my body didn't seem to realize it as I braced for impact.

The car made it through fine, though, and the area we were in now looked the same as the garage we'd come through, only there were only two cars now—a sleek black Corvette and a black Range Rover. My chest panged thinking about how Theo would have oohed and ahhed over the Corvette.

Ethan parked the SUV beside it and we all sat there for a moment.

It'd only been three days since we'd fled the manor, but it felt like a lifetime ago.

This car had become our safe place since then, and leaving its confines felt foreign and wrong.

I felt lost without Theo, like I couldn't do this, but I knew had to.

"Well, we're here," Ethan said unnecessarily.

None of us made a move to get out.

After the days on the road, the fear of even stopping too long, it didn't feel right that now we were somewhere safe.

And really, *nothing* was safe.

We would be idiots to let our guard down. The three of us didn't know Jee, and I hated to say it, but we really didn't even know Ethan. Theo had trusted him, though, and that counted for something.

"You said this guy is paranoid," Winston started. "Are you sure he's not going to attack us for showing up?"

"We'll be fine," Ethan assured, pulling the key from the ignition.

We filed out of the vehicle and I slung my backpack on and grabbed Nigel into my arms. He meowed and I buried my face into his fur.

"I miss him too, buddy," I whispered, a crack in my voice.

The three of us followed Ethan to a metal door. There was a pad where he placed his hand. It scanned it and then a robotic voice spoke, "Welcome back, Mr. Hunter."

The door slung open and I gaped. The door was at least a foot thick.

"It prevents weapons or even magic from being able to penetrate it," Ethan exclaimed.

Adelaide gagged. "Please, let's not use the word *penetrate*. Kay?"

Ethan shook his head and chuckled. "Just get in here."

We strolled down a narrow hall, both sides lined with cinderblock walls like in the garage.

Poor Winston and Adelaide were still in their formal wear. Since we were keeping our stops to a minimum Ethan hadn't let them go in a store to get something else.

The hallway ended with an elevator. It was one of those industrial ones that you opened and shut yourself.

We piled onto it and Ethan pushed the button to send us up.

The elevator made a noise that didn't sound good at all to me and lurched upward.

I grabbed onto Winston's arm to steady myself as I lost my balance.

He glanced at me and I quickly let go of his arm, mumbling an apology under my breath.

The elevator stopped on the top floor—well, I assumed it was the top since it took forever to get there—and Ethan opened the door.

"Ethan?" a voice called out questioningly.

"It's me," Ethan replied as the four of us stepped out.

Jee rounded the corner and stopped when he saw all of us. He stared for a moment, blinking his dark eyes at us. He was insanely tall, with floppy black hair and cheekbones that could cut ice. "What the hell?"

Ethan stepped toward him, his hands outstretched. "I wouldn't have brought them here if it wasn't important. The safe house in Seattle was attacked. Mara is a Chosen One, and she needs our protection. I knew this would be the safest place for her."

Jee peered around Ethan to look at me, and I waved awkwardly.

I hated being the center of attention.

Jee sighed loudly. "What about those two?" He wrinkled his nose at Adelaide and Winston like they were worse than scum stuck to his shoe. I was beginning to wonder how Ethan had ever met this guy, let alone fallen in love with him, because he seemed entirely *un*lovable.

"They're my friends, I trust them."

Jee appeared skeptical and not at all appeased, but he nodded. "Fine. You all need to shower. You smell like death and tootsie rolls and tootsie rolls are *gross*."

Jee narrowed his eyes at me. Well, not at *me* but at the glaring cat in my arms.

"Oh, for fuck's sake you brought a cat here too? Let's open up the place for all the woodland creatures. We'll join hands and sing songs while they clean my apartment."

Ethan sighed and grabbed Jee's hand. "Calm down, you won't even know he's here."

Nigel chose that moment to jump out of my arms and walk over to Jee, brushing against his legs.

"Won't know he's here my ass," Jee mumbled.

Winston cleared his throat. "I'd really love that shower right now."

Jee sighed. "There are two upstairs. You'll have to take turns." He swished his hands, blue sparks flickering at the tips. "There are fresh clothes waiting for you too."

Ethan shook his head. "Where'd you steal those from?"

Jee shrugged. "They won't be missed."

Jee and Ethan disappeared into the apartment and out of our sight.

"You guys go ahead," I told Winston and Adelaide.

"Nah, ladies first," Winston objected.

"I insist. I know you have to be ready to get out of your tux."

He chuckled. "You've got that right, love. Fine, I'll accept this time."

The set of steps was to our right and the two of them headed up, Adelaide looking at me over her shoulder before she disappeared from sight.

I moved through the apartment, checking it out. The floors were old worn oak, and the ceilings were high with industrial piping. I found Ethan and Jee in the kitchen, laughing about something. The kitchen was small, with gray cabinetry and stainless-steel countertops. Across from it was the open living space with a large gray sectional, TV, and an art easel.

On the easel was a half-finished painting and I moved toward it as if drawn by an invisible force. The painting wasn't finished, but the colors were dark. Grays, and browns, almost depressing in quality. It looked like the starts of a basement, or maybe a cellar.

"Jee paints what he sees," Ethan explained beside me, scaring me since I hadn't heard him approach.

"It's so I don't crazy," Jee added, stepping up to my other side. "Well, *crazier* than I already am." He shrugged like it was no big deal, clasping his hands behind his back.

"What's this one?" I asked.

He shrugged and shoved his hands into the pockets of his jeans. "I'm not sure yet. That's how most of them start, muted with no clear picture, but by the time I'm done it makes sense."

I turned to him. "Does it get tiring? Knowing so much?"

He pressed his lips together and thought for a moment. "Only when it's something bad. I don't like knowing it's coming. There's usually nothing I, nor anyone else, can do to stop it. It is what is—the gift of knowing the future isn't so I or anyone else can change it. It's so we can prepare for the inevitable."

"How often do you know something good?"

"Not often enough." His dark eyes got a far away look to them.

I couldn't imagine how difficult it must be to know things and not be able to do anything about it. I'd think you'd go mad with the knowledge.

I heard the telltale screeching of shower pipes as the water cut off.

"Looks like it's my turn."

I excused myself and headed upstairs. There was a long hall extending in both directions, with railing on one side overlooking the downstairs.

A door on the right side opened and I turned that way.

"Oh," I stuttered when Winston stepped out in nothing but a towel.

His body was damp, and his hair hung down into his eyes.

My cheeks heated, and I took a step back. "S-Sorry." I looked down at the floor. For some odd reason I felt like I was cheating on Theo by even looking at Winston, which was stupid because it wasn't like I was looking at him in *that* way.

I flicked my eyes back up to him and he shoved his hair out of his eyes, a smirk lifting the edges of his lips.

"Bathroom's all yours, love." He passed by me and into a bedroom.

I closed my eyes and took a breath before moving down the hall. I found the room with my fresh clothes and Nigel was already curled on the bed like he knew where to go. There was another set of clothes for Adelaide.

Grabbing up the clothes, I quickly scratched Nigel behind the ears before heading into the bathroom. I locked the door behind me and set my clothes on the counter.

I braced my hands on the counter, and forced my eyes to my reflection.

Dark circles engulfed my eyes, giving me an almost skeletal appearance. Even my cheeks were hallow and gaunt.

I still felt sick we'd left Theo behind—sealed his fate.

It wasn't fair.

Forcing myself away from the mirror I turned on the shower and stripped off my clothes, leaving them in a pile on the floor.

I pushed the curtain aside and stepped into the shower, pulling it closed behind me.

I stood beneath the spray, letting it drench me, and wished it could wash and cleanse me of my sins. Realistically, I knew nothing was strong enough to do that.

My chin began to wobble and soon the tears fell.

Theo.

His eyes.

His smile.

His laugh.

His sarcastic and smart-ass remarks.

All things I'd never hear or see again

I'd thought I'd known what it was like to have my heart break with all the times Theo had pushed me away, but losing him like this had brought the most unimaginable pain. Like someone had shoved their hand through my chest and carved out part of my heart. Somehow, I was still able to live, but I was different. I was harder, less feeling, I lacked empathy.

All that mattered now was making sure the Iniquitous paid for this.

I knew I was in no way prepared to take them on now, but I wanted to. I'd prepare myself, train, and learn my magic, and when the time came I'd hunt down every last one of them.

I wouldn't let Theo's story end here.

I wouldn't let him be simply another enchanter gone too soon to the Iniquitous.

No, he'd be the catalyst to the war no enchanter wanted but needed if they wanted to survive.

And when it was over, I'd make sure *no one* ever forgot his name.

chapter four

I SAT ON THE END OF the bed brushing my damp hair. It was a matted and tangled mess from days in the car and even half a bottle of conditioner hadn't been able to save it.

"Hey," Adelaide said softly, slipping into the room.

Her own hair was braided to the side, and she wore the same pair of sweatpants and t-shirt I did. Apparently, Jee couldn't have conjured—well, I guess *stolen* was a better term—something more stylish. Not that it mattered. Nothing really did to me right then.

"Are you hungry?" she asked, and I noticed the plates in her hand, one for her and one for me.

I started to shake my head but nodded instead. I *had* to eat. Skipping meals was only hurting me.

I laid my brush down beside me and took a plate from her. She sat down beside me, curling her legs up onto the bed.

"I'm sorry we have to share a bed." She picked up a piece of garlic bread from her plate and dipped it in her spaghetti.

I laughed lightly. "It's not a big deal. It's only a bed."

"I know, but I'm sure you'd rather have your space."

I looked at her, seeing the sadness I knew I possessed in my eyes reflected in hers.

"You miss him too, not just me. We're better off together."

She nodded and looked down at her plate. I forced myself to twist some spaghetti around my fork and take a bite. It wasn't bad.

"I ... I know he died doing what he was always meant to do, but it still hurts losing him," she admitted. "But I'm proud too."

"I'm sorry he had to die because of me," I admitted.

That was what hurt me most. He stayed behind and took them on because of *me*. Because he was my protector and it was what he was *meant* to do.

She shook her head. "It's what he was supposed to do, and he loved you. He would've done it anyway. That's Theodore."

It didn't escape my notice she was now talking about him in the past tense. I didn't call her out on it, though, because I knew it was for the best.

We both had to move on, even if it was hard, *especially* then.

"I have to grow stronger. I need to be strong enough to take them on."

"Oh, Mara," she breathed. "Don't do anything stupid."

"It's not like I'm going to take them on right now. Theo might've been working with me, but I know I'm not that good yet. I have to get better."

I wished I was further along in my training, but the fact was I wasn't and my age hindered me too. As enchanters grew older their magic grew stronger.

Adelaide stared at her plate for a moment. "You know I'm with you. I won't let you fight this battle alone. We're stronger together."

"You don't have to," I whispered. I knew Ethan, Winston, and Adelaide said they'd fight with me, but this wasn't their battle. I didn't expect them to be a part of this. They could *die,* and that information was enough to send anyone running in the opposite direction.

"I've been sheltered my whole life, behind those walls. I refuse to continue doing nothing while others suffer. It's wrong, and I'd never forgive myself. They killed Theodore, but think about how many others they've killed." She flicked her hair out of her eyes, the dark blue color swirling with determination. "But how will we know where to find them?"

"I don't know. We just will."

I knew it in my gut we'd find them. We had to.

My desire for vengeance was getting out of hand, but without it I feared I'd fall apart. It was all I had now.

I finished my food and took Adelaide's plate when she was done.

The apartment was quiet, almost eerily so, and since it was unfamiliar I found myself glancing over my shoulder at every turn.

I padded down the stairs and into the kitchen, washing our plates in the sink.

"I thought you weren't going to come down."

I jumped back from the sink, splashing water on myself in the process.

"You scared me," I breathed, placing a hand to my racing heart.

"I'm sorry." Jee stepped out of the shadows, his hands clasped behind his back.

"Oh my God." I brought my hand to my mouth.

His eyes were leached of color. They were all white like his eyes had rolled into the back of his head.

"Jee?" I prompted, and he tilted his head.

"The shadows say you're going to save us. Is it true Light One?"

My heart thundered in my ears. I wanted to run, but something urged me to stay where I was.

"I-I don't know," I stuttered. "Everyone tells me I have a purpose, that I'm *chosen*, but I don't think I'm special."

He clucked his tongue and moved around the counter, coming closer to me.

I edged back and he stopped.

"Are you afraid?"

"No."

His tongue slipped out between his lips and back in. "You are. I taste it."

"You taste it? You taste my fear? Like in the air?"

"I see things, but I also know things."

"Isn't it the same thing?"

He chuckled. "Not at all."

Oookay then.

"My abilities extend beyond seeing the future. That's just..." He paused, flicking his fingers. "A party trick."

"Hardly seems like a party trick to me. Why are your eyes like that?"

His lips twitched. "I'm *seeing*. You interrupted me."

"Oh." I flicked my head toward the painting. "Can I see?

He shrugged. "Maybe you can make sense of it. I don't seem to understand."

I moved toward the painting and saw he'd finished it.

It wasn't clear, almost abstract, but I recognized the stone walls of the manor.

"That's Victor," I breathed. "On the ground there." A tall looming figure stood over him, fingertips flickering with a rainbow of colors and a sword in the other hand. I stared at the hooded profile of the figure. The body shape and commanding presence reminded me of Theo, but it couldn't be. "Finn," I gasped. "That's Finn."

Jee made a noise in his throat. "I'm happy someone understands."

I watched as the white in his eyes disappeared and returned to normal.

"I'm sorry I scared you." He shrugged, but his tone told me he was hardly sorry. I got the impression Jee didn't care for anyone—except apparently Ethan—and definitely didn't care what anyone thought of him. There was something sort of freeing about being that way.

I laughed and shook my head. "I'm sure you are."

He cracked a smile. "You're right, I'm not."

"I should get to bed."

He mock bowed. "Sleep well, my queen."

He bled into the shadows and disappeared from sight.

I headed back upstairs to the room I was sharing with Adelaide. She was already under the covers fast asleep.

Her dark hair fanned around her head and her lips were parted as she breathed peacefully.

I doubted I could sleep like that, and I felt slightly envious.

Slipping into the bed, I laid on my back, staring up at the ceiling.

"Wherever you are," I whispered softly, "know I love you. I always will. And this ... this is not the end."

When I closed my eyes it felt like a pair of lips were pressed to the corner of mine, but when I opened them, no one was there.

chapter five

Sun shone into the apartment, reflecting the shadows of the windowpanes onto the living room floors.

"I'm not a bed and breakfast. You make your own beds and your own damn food," Jee ranted from the couch, poring over a sketchbook, his charcoal pencil moving madly.

"No one suggested you were." Winston grabbed an apple and took a large bite.

"Food isn't free either," Jee grumbled.

"In case you hadn't noticed, we're kind of on the run and broke," I snapped.

He glanced at me. "What's got your panties in the bunch this morning?"

"Nothing," I muttered, and moved into the kitchen searching for some cereal.

I finally found some under the sink. Who put cereal under the sink?

I grabbed a box of Frosted Flakes and found a bowl in a drawer. Jee had an interesting way of organizing his stuff.

"You want some?" I asked Adelaide as she slid onto one of the barstools. Her hair was a tangled mess, but she looked rested at least.

She nodded. "Is there coffee too?"

"Stay out of my coffee," Jee warned.

"Don't listen to him," Ethan said, strolling into the room. He tugged a shirt on and glanced at Jee. "He likes to mess with people."

"Maybe I don't like people in my space using my stuff. Did you ever think of that?"

Ethan sighed. "Drink all the coffee you want. I'll buy more."

"Well as long as you're buying." Jee chuckled as Ethan sat down beside him. Ethan kissed his cheek and I'd swear Jee blushed.

I fixed Adelaide a bowl of cereal and gave it to her before starting on the coffee. When it was ready, I poured the two of us mugs and sat beside her to eat. Winston had hopped up on the corner of the counter, finishing his apple.

Adelaide took a sip of her coffee, her eyes closed with a look of pleasure on her face.

"Now I can start my morning."

I shook my head at her and ate my cereal.

"What are we doing today?" I asked no one in particular.

Ethan and Jee exchanged a look.

"I need to start learning," I pleaded with Ethan. "There's so much more I need to know."

Theo had done his best to train me, and I knew I was ahead of other enchanters my age because of it, but I also wasn't dumb enough to think I couldn't learn more.

I *had* to learn more if I had any chance of defeating them.

They were stronger, faster, ruthless.

They didn't care about killing, and I ... I did.

I had to let that part of myself go.

I had to become like *them*.

Well, not one of them, but I had to let go of my sensitivities.

"I know," Ethan agreed. I knew there was a but coming. "*But* we don't know how safe it is here yet. I don't want you out in the open, practicing magic, and draw them in unaware."

"I thought they couldn't go out in the day?"

"They can't, but they can still sense your presence if they're near."

"Wouldn't they be everywhere, though? You know, like in all cities?"

He shook his head. "They're not plentiful like you'd think. Yes, they're powerful and they've hurt a number of enchanters, killed them, but there's not many and they stick together."

Again, I wondered why no one had tried to fight them before. It seemed like an easy win to me, but I also realized I was a newbie in this world. I didn't know what all kind of damage they'd done. Fear paralyzed you, and it seemed to me like most enchanters were terrified of them.

"I promise I'll train you, Mara," Ethan promised. "You too, Adelaide. But I won't do anything that might risk your safety."

I nodded. I understood, I did, but it didn't mean I liked it.

"Why can't we train here?" I asked.

Jee glared at me. "I won't have untrained enchanters burning down my house so don't even go there."

"What about hand to hand combat?" I pestered. "I want to learn to use a sword too."

Ethan tilted his head toward Jee with a questioning look. "Fine! You can use my training room, but *no* magic in there, got it? Take all magic outside these walls," he gestured madly.

"You use magic," I countered, messing with him.

"Yes, because I'm old enough. So is Ethan."

"So am I." Winston raised his hand and I shot him a glare. He slowly lowered his hand.

"See—" Jee pointed to the three of them "—we can use magic properly. But I won't let you two go running amok."

"Is this the part where I chant 'amok, amok'?" I asked, and the three of them stared at me.

"No magic," Jee warned again.

I sighed. I wouldn't argue further because after the library fiasco with Theo and tumbling all the books to the floor I didn't want to risk something happening and pissing off Jee. He wouldn't think twice about kicking us out and right now he, and his apartment, were all we had to keep us safe.

"When can we start the other training?" I asked Ethan.

He shrugged. "Today, I guess. I don't see why not."

My heart soared with excitement. It wasn't magic, but it was something. Something to keep me busy, and something that would get me one step closer to being able to take down Thaddeus and his loons. For a moment, I pictured myself piercing the heart of one of the Iniquitous and before the light left their eyes telling them they were dying because they took Theo from me.

"Can I get in on this?" Winston asked. "I'm not proficient with a sword, and I'm not the best at hand to hand either."

"Sure. We'll start after lunch. Jee and I will go scout the surrounding area for anywhere safe to practice magic."

"We will?" Jee looked none too thrilled at being volunteered for this adventure.

"Yes, we will," Ethan bit out and stood up, dragging Jee with him.

The sketchpad fell to the floor with a thump and I heard a hiss from beneath the couch. I guessed Nigel didn't like having his beauty sleep disturbed.

Ethan and Jee headed out, and the three of us were silent until we couldn't hear the elevator clacking anymore.

Winston let out a breath. "This is crazy. I can't believe we're here."

"I know what you mean," I agreed.

It all still felt like a bad dream I was waiting to wake up from, but no matter how hard I tried, I couldn't wake up.

"Do you think we're safe here?" Adelaide asked softly, pushing her cereal around the bowl. "I mean, Ethan trusts this guy but he's a little ... odd."

"He's definitely different," I agreed. "I'm not sure he's entirely enchanter."

"What do you mean?" Winston hopped off the counter and came over to lean against the overhang of the island where Adelaide and I sat.

I shrugged and pushed my bowl away. I'd actually managed to eat all of it, so I was impressed.

"I came down last night to clean our plates." I pointed to Adelaide. "And he stepped out of the shadows. It was like he was actually a part of them if

46

that makes any sense. His eyes too ... there was no color. He said it was because he was *seeing*, but ... I didn't believe him."

Winston pressed his lips together. "We'll all keep our eyes open, okay? The minute something seems bad we're out of here."

"What about Ethan?" Adelaide asked.

"If we can't trust Jee, can we trust him?" he reasoned.

Adelaide bit her lip. "I guess you're right."

It sucked, but it was true. We had to be careful with everything we said and did.

Even with each other.

Anybody could be working for the other side.

Anybody.

chapter six

I T SEEMED LIKE AN AGONIZING wait for Jee and Ethan to return to the loft.

But once they were back we got right down to business.

Ethan handed me a sword, then Adelaide and Winston, off the wall.

I was impressed with Jee's training room. It was well-equipped with workout equipment, weapons, and even a rock-climbing wall.

Ethan cleared his throat and grabbed a sword off the wall for himself.

"When fighting with a sword, be aware of your surroundings. In other words, pay attention." He zeroed in on Adelaide who stood looking at the intricate work on the hilt of the sword he'd given her. When she didn't get the hint he cleared his throat again.

Her head jolted up.

"Huh?"

"Like I said, pay attention. A strike can come from anywhere." He balanced his sword on the palms of his hands. "You want a sword that balances you. If it's too heavy for you, you're not going to be able to fight properly. And when you're fighting, *relax;* a tense body is not good for fighting. You need to be loose so your movements are fluid."

"Anything else, oh wise one?" Winston asked.

In a lightning fast move, Ethan had the tip of the sword pushed against Winston's throat. Ethan tilted his head, fighting a smile. "Yes. Don't ever engage in a fight you know you can't win. Use magic, or run."

Winston swallowed and the smallest trickle of blood glided down his pale throat. My eyes focused on it, as if drawn to the scarlet color like a moth to a flame.

It called to me, the blood lust. How I itched to see the Iniquitous slain at my feet.

Ethan pulled his sword back. "I want each of you to spar with me so I can see where you're at and what we need to work on. You first."

"Me?" Adelaide squeaked.

He nodded.

Winston and I moved away, sitting against the back wall.

Ethan circled Adelaide on the mat, and fear shone in her eyes.

"Adelaide, you've got this," I called out to her.

Ethan lifted his sword, and it arced through the air.

She screamed and ran away.

Ethan choked out a chuckle. "Well, at least you realized you couldn't win. We'll start at the beginning with you. Winston." He flicked his fingers, signaling Winston to stand and join him.

Adelaide scurried to my side and slid down the wall to sit on the floor.

"I'm so going to suck at this," she grumbled.

"You'll get it," I assured her. "I'll practice with you too. I'm not the best so I'll be more on your level."

"At least you know some things." She sighed and pushed her hair out of her eyes. It fell right back down and she pulled it back, securing it with an elastic off her wrist.

"It's easy to pick up. You'll learn quick."

"I hope you're right." She stretched her legs out. "I feel so unprepared."

I knew what she meant. I felt that way too. I didn't see how I'd ever be capable taking on one Iniquitous, let alone an army of them. But I had to get to that point, because I didn't think anyone else would fight this battle. Maybe it was my purpose, why I was a Chosen One. I wondered how you finally *knew* your purpose or if it happened without you even realizing it.

That seemed anti-climactic and suckish.

The sound of clashing swords pulled me from my thoughts.

Winston was surprisingly proficient with a sword. I wasn't expecting that, and I didn't know why exactly.

Ethan jutted his sword toward Winston's abdomen, and Winston jumped away, stealthy like a cat.

Nigel would approve.

The guys sparred for so long they were both drenched in sweat when they called it a draw.

"Your turn." Ethan pointed his sword at me.

"Wish me luck," I joked with Adelaide, but she didn't even crack a smile.

I stretched my legs, stiff from sitting so long, and stood in front of Ethan.

"Ready?" he asked.

I nodded.

In the blink of an eye he swung his sword in my direction. I blocked it easily, a smile on my face.

This felt good.

It felt *normal*.

Ethan chuckled and took a step back. "Nice."

"Thanks." I took a stab in his direction and his sword clashed with mine.

And so began our dance.

Ethan swung his sword toward my head.

Duck, a voice whispered faintly inside my mind.

I nearly froze from the sound of the voice but instead I listened, almost on instinct.

Theo? I questioned. The voice had been a weak gasp, it could've been anyone, but it was like my soul had finally awakened from where it had lay dormant for days.

Silence echoed inside my skull.

I wanted to find the voice, to know if it was real or my imagination, but I couldn't lose focus.

Ethan and I fought hard, like he had with Winston.

We seemed to glide effortlessly along the floor, neither of us gaining the upper hand, until ...

"You're dead." I held the tip of my sword to his heart.

He chuckled and dropped his sword to the ground. "Theodore's taught you well."

I hung my sword back on the wall where he'd gotten it from. "He tried."

All the hours we'd put in, at the time I hated ... well, maybe not hated, since I got one on one time with him, but it hadn't been all rainbows and sunshine. It'd been hard. He put me through the wringer. I was glad for it now.

"That's it for today. We'll hit it hard tomorrow after breakfast."

"What?" My face fell. "But ..."

Ethan shook his head. "We already sparred for forty minutes, Mara. Your body needs to rest."

"It was that long?" It hadn't seemed longer than ten minutes. During the time when we'd been sparring I hadn't been able to think about anything else. It'd been nice to have a reprieve from my constantly racing thoughts.

He stared at me for a moment, as if puzzling something out. "Yes," he said, but it came out sounding more like a question.

I shook my head. "How am I ever going to be prepared if you quit after that?" Anger bubbled inside me—anger at Ethan for wanting to quit so soon, anger at Theo being gone, anger at the Iniquitous and Thaddeus and all they'd destroyed.

"Mara," Adelaide said softly, trying to calm me down.

"Theo's *dead*," I reminded them like they didn't already know. "And how many other enchanters died that night? Our friends? Our professors? You guys might be content with this but I'm not. I have to do something, and this isn't enough. You're not *trying*," I seethed. I could feel my blood boiling and it wasn't good. When my temper rose I couldn't control my magic as well. The last thing I needed was it bursting forth and causing a problem. "We have to *fight* and we can't do that if we're not learning."

Ethan held his ground. "I'm done for the day. Feel free to stay in here and work off your aggression." His eyes flashed with irritation at me pushing him and I guess, in a way, calling him weak.

But he had to know I was right. We'd never get anywhere if this was all we did and stopped.

He picked up his sword from the floor, returned it, and strode from the room like he didn't have a care in the world.

Adelaide and Winston stared at me, waiting for me to say something.

"Just go," I finally whispered.

Adelaide hesitated and then left.

Winston took several careful steps toward me. "It's okay to be angry, or sad, but don't take it out on us. We're your friends. We're here for you."

I clenched my teeth. "I saw him ... I saw him *murdered*." Tears began to stream down my cheeks. "Only days ago, might I add. I'm sorry if I'm not coping well."

Winston raised his hands in surrender. "Sorry, you're right. Forget I said anything."

He too left, and I was finally alone.

I sunk to the floor on the squishy mat and lay down on my back.

I listened carefully to the buzzing of my mind, searching for the voice.

Theo? Is that you? Are you there?

Silence.

Theo, please, if that's you say something. Do something. I'm begging you. Please.

Nothing.

I felt my throat grow thick and my heart constrict.

I must've imagined the voice it was my only explanation.

Staring up at the ceiling I crossed my hands over my chest as sadness consumed me. I was so desperate for my connection with Theo I was now hearing his voice in my head.

It was official—I was insane.

I sat up and glanced at the rock-climbing wall. The others might think what we did today was enough, but it wasn't. Nothing would be. Even if we trained all day long every day, which wouldn't be possible, we still wouldn't be ready.

I didn't think anything could actually prepare you for the Iniquitous.

They had nothing to lose, and we had everything to fight for.

Standing up, I headed over to the rock-climbing wall. There was chalk to help you hold on and I rubbed my hands into it.

I'd never done this before, but something urged me on.

To grow stronger, I needed more than sword play.

I needed to strengthen my whole body.

I inhaled a breath and let it out slowly, then grabbed onto the first formation.

The wall was high, at least for a home. It had to be twenty feet tall.

Hefting my body up the wall, I grunted as I worked. From the floor this had looked easy, but now it was clear to me it wasn't easy at all. It took not only incredible upper body strength, but all-over strength as well.

My foot slid off one of the purchases and I scrambled to hold on, my belly pressing into the wall painfully as I winced. I found a place for my foot and took a breath before ascending again.

I was new at this, and weak, so it took me a while to climb all the way up and back down.

By the time my feet touched the floor I was exhausted.

My limbs were jittery, shaking from the effort it'd taken to lug my body up the wall. I was going to be sore tomorrow, which wouldn't be good for training, but at the same time this was what I needed. I needed to get stronger and I couldn't do it by sitting on my ass all day.

I collapsed onto the mats once more, lying on my back with my arms and legs spread like I was making a snow angel.

My lips quirked with remembrance of how Theo had never built a snowman. The ache returned to my chest. It went away for a little while at times, but it always came back.

It was unavoidable; like rain, or snow, it was one of those things that always happened eventually.

"You're still in here?"

I sat up to find Winston standing in the doorway.

"Yeah, I wanted some time to myself to think."

It was mostly true.

He nodded. "Jee and Ethan are out again. I thought you might like to know."

"Thanks."

He hesitated a moment longer and then shoved away from the door and disappeared.

I stood up and stretched my legs and then my arms above my head. I knew I couldn't stay in here forever, and I desperately needed a shower.

I headed down the hall and stopped near the stairs, spying Adelaide and Winston watching TV.

It shouldn't, but it aggravated me they were so blasé about everything.

Life went on, I supposed.

I should have been glad they were acting normal, that Adelaide wasn't constantly crying or blaming me, but still I wanted ... I guessed, I wanted to know they hurt like I did. Being alone with my grief was a painful thought and a burden I didn't want to bear.

That probably made me selfish.

I forced myself up the stairs and showered the grimy sweat from my body. When I stepped into our room after, I found two piles of clothes conjured for each of us. I'd had some clothes stuffed into my backpack, but not enough, so this was a welcome relief. I didn't need to be worrying about what I was going to wear when there were more important things at hand.

I dressed and sat on the bed for a moment, soaking in the quiet.

My mind wandered back to Victor and his final words.

Who was Cleo?

I'd never heard the name before he'd spoken it. It meant absolutely nothing to me, but it had to be important for it to be the last thing he said.

I knew one person who might know who Cleo was, or could at least figure it out, and that was Jee.

But I still wasn't sure I could trust him. He rubbed me the wrong way, but it could be because he was different. Different wasn't a bad thing, but in my situation I had to watch my back.

I groaned and stood up, carrying my towel back to the bathroom to hang it on the door.

I couldn't hide from everyone all day, but social interaction was the last thing I wanted to do.

Ethan and Jee hadn't returned yet, at least from what I could see as I descended the steps, and Winston and Adelaide were still in front of the TV, but now they had snacks.

"What are you guys watching?" I asked, sitting beside Adelaide.

"Stephen Amell shirtless," she replied, staring at the TV and absentmindedly eating popcorn.

Winston groaned. "It's called *Arrow*, love."

"Do I look like I care?" she intoned, not removing her gaze from the TV.

I watched as the guy did some sort of ladder thing with a pole. It looked difficult, but he didn't seem to be hurting.

"I'm going to get a drink." I popped up. Sitting still was becoming increasingly difficult. I needed to dispel this restless energy.

I hated being jittery and on edge all the time.

It had to be because Theo wasn't there. Something about his presence calmed me. Maybe it was because he was my protector, or maybe it was just *him*.

My body sensed his absence, and it was none too happy about it.

I opened the refrigerator, searched the items, and closed it before opening it again and grabbing the orange juice bottle. I poured a glass and swished it around, watching the liquid like it was the most fascinating thing I'd ever seen.

"You're supposed to drink that."

I jumped at the sound of Jee's voice and dropped the glass.

It shattered at my feet in a million small pieces, the sticky liquid coating my feet and toes, some splashing up onto the fabric of my stretchy leggings.

"You have got to stop scaring me," I scolded him.

"Don't move," Ethan warned. "I'll clean this up. I don't want you to step in glass by accident."

I didn't want to listen to him, but I stood still anyway.

He grabbed a dustpan and brush, plus a rag, and went to work.

Jee leaned his elbow on the counter and his head on his hand, watching Ethan.

Winston and Adelaide peered over the back of the couch watching too.

"You okay over there?" Winston asked with a wry grin.

I gave him an okay gesture. "A-okay."

Ethan got all the glass picked up and mopped up the orange juice the best he could.

I stepped back and winced. *"Ow."*

"Shit did I miss a piece?" he asked.

I lifted my right foot and a small piece of glass stuck out of it. It was barely half an inch in size, but already blood oozed around it.

"I'm so sorry," Ethan looked up at me panicked.

"It's okay, just pull it out."

He grabbed the glass and pulled it out carefully.

I winced at the sting.

"You okay?"

I nodded and hopped up onto the counter, sticking my foot into the sink so I could rinse off the juice and blood.

"Great, now she's sticking her dirty foot in my sink," Jee grumbled. "I hate house crashers."

Ethan sighed. "I had no where else to bring them."

Jee grinned in response. "I like to give you shit."

I shook my head and cleaned my foot. I didn't know how much longer I could stand being in this place—Jee was something else, but I wasn't sure trying to make a go of it on my own would be the safest thing. Plus, I'd never forgive myself for leaving Adelaide behind.

"Stay up there until I know I've gotten everything," Ethan warned me.

He disappeared down the hall and returned with a small vacuum.

There was the telltale crunch of small pieces getting sucked up into it.

"You know," I intoned, looking at Jee, "this wouldn't have happened if you hadn't snuck up on me."

His lips lifted into the smallest smile. "Or maybe you should pay better attention to your surroundings."

I couldn't argue with him there. If Jee had been able to sneak up on me, who else might?

"I think you're safe," Ethan announced, and I hopped down.

"How's the scouting going?"

He shrugged. "So far so good. We haven't sensed anyone and we found a good wooded area, away from the city and any people, that'll be perfect for practicing. I want to give it a good couple of weeks though, maybe longer, of nothing worrisome before we venture out."

My shoulders sagged.

"I know it sucks," he added. "But better safe than sorry."

I pressed my lips together and nodded. I wasn't happy about it, but he was right. Theo had risked his life for me, for us, and I couldn't throw that away by doing what I wanted. I needed to listen, and wait, instead of springing into action.

I started to leave the kitchen, and Ethan grabbed my arm to stop me.

"Do you want more juice?" he asked.

I shook my head. I didn't know why I wanted it in the first place.

A distraction, maybe?

Wasn't that what everything was these days?

chapter seven

S WEAT GLIDED DOWN MY FACE, dripping off my chin. My hair was plastered with dampness and my arms shook from holding a heavy sword for so long, not to mention fighting with it.

Ethan was a skilled swordsman.

He was fast, almost unrealistically fast. I didn't know how I was able to match his moves so easily. It was like something inside me had taken over and I was along for the ride. His sword clashed against mine and the force reverberated up my arm, making my muscles quake.

I wanted to cry, to give in and beg him to end this, but my stubborn side refused to let me give up.

Ethan too was drenched in sweat and I could see he was tiring as well.

But the question was, could I outlast him?

Adelaide and Winston sat off to the side against the wall watching. I was barely aware of their presence. I couldn't be, not when all my focus needed to be on this, the next strike, where I needed to move my feet and arms.

I kept wondering if I'd hear the voice again, Theo's voice, but so far nothing.

It made me wonder if I'd only imagined it before, an illusion conjured by my mind.

The mind was funny like that. It liked to give you things, give you *hope*, and then snatch it away.

Theo was gone, but if I could hear his voice ... it might be enough.

Ethan groaned and pushed harder. He was encroaching on my space, wanting to back me into a corner, get past my defense.

With a huff, I pushed back, our swords clashing.

The sound of metal against metal was music to my ears.

Ethan stumbled over his feet in tiredness, and one slip up was enough.

The tip of my sword pressed into his throat and he halted, his eyes wide. He looked like he needed to swallow, but if he did the sword would pierce his throat. Not enough to kill him, of course, but he would bleed.

"I win," I gasped, shoving damp strands of hair from my eyes. They'd come loose from my ponytail and had been driving me nuts, but I persisted.

I lowered my sword and he shook his head. "I shouldn't be surprised and yet I am. You're pretty remarkable."

I glowed from his praise. Theo had trained me hard, and while he praised me, it wasn't often and usually in his own gruff ways.

Though there were times when the pride literally ignited him—like when he was teaching me magic.

He'd been so proud then.

I wished he could see me now, how hard I was fighting.

For him.

Because of him.

It was always about him.

"Thank you," I finally said. "I like sparring with you."

He chuckled. "I think you're better than me. Maybe you need to be teaching all of us."

I shrugged. "I'm not that good, not yet, but I like it. It's easy for me."

"Mara's a bad ass," Adelaide exclaimed. "*Bad ass,*" she added with inflection.

I shook my head, trying to hide my smile.

"I'm not surprised," Winston started. "She has that look about her."

"What kind of look?" I asked breathless. I wasn't sure I was ever going to catch my breath again.

"A huntress."

"A huntress," I repeated softly under my breath.

I'd never thought of myself that way. I always thought I was weak, and somehow less because I'd always thought I was human, like somehow that fact meant I was behind everybody else.

But maybe I was wrong.

Maybe I was *stronger* for it, because it made me work harder, fight longer.

I hung up my sword on the wall and fanned my tank top to cool my skin.

"How long did we go?" I asked Winston.

He glanced at his watch. "An hour."

"Damn," I cursed.

I couldn't believe I'd held out this long. I guessed my stubborn streak wasn't such a bad thing after all. Without it, I would've given up ages ago.

My arms felt like Jell-O, my shoulders ached, and my legs shook ready to give out at any second.

I glanced at Ethan, and he looked as bad off as me.

He too was drenched in sweat, and the veins in his arms stood out in stark contrast against his skin. His hair was damp and pushed away from his eyes. He glanced at me, cracking a smile as he tried to catch his breath.

As much as I wanted to start practicing more with magic, I couldn't deny this was therapeutic in a way.

I also knew magic couldn't win every fight.

After all, magic didn't kill Theo, a sword to the stomach did.

"I know one thing," Winston started with a wry smile, "I never want to get in a fight with Mara."

I chuckled but it came out as a strangled sound since I still hadn't caught my breath.

"I'm hitting the shower," Ethan announced, hanging up his sword as well. He glanced down at me, his hair falling into his eyes. "You did good."

"Thank you."

I still had the feeling like nothing I did was going to be good enough, but at the end of the day I had to keep at it.

For me.

For Theo.

For this world.

"I don't know how you do it." Adelaide shook her head. "I *suck* at this."

"It's only been two days," I reminded her. "And yesterday doesn't even count."

She frowned. "I feel like I'm letting my brother down. He was so skilled at this kind of thing and I'm ... not."

"It's not easy, but you'll get it. I know you will. And it's not like he was perfect at it overnight. I'm sure he would've loved for all of us to think that, but he had to learn it too."

She sighed. "I hope you're right. I'm not as sure."

"Theo's been training me for months," I paused, and swallowed. "He *was* training me for months. I have a leg up on you. He really focused on hand to hand combat more than swords, but it's helped."

Theo had made sure I learned to read my opponent like an open book, and he'd been right. If you knew what to look for you could find weak spots.

All you needed was to find one weak spot to gain the upper hand.

"I'll help you if you want," I told her.

She lit up. "Really?"

I didn't know why she was so shocked. "Yeah, of course. We can start tomorrow. I'm exhausted."

Training with Adelaide and Ethan would definitely help build my endurance. Plus, maybe I'd get through to Adelaide better. When she fought with Ethan she basically squeaked and ducked. She was intimidated by him. I understood why, too. He was tall and muscular, and he was a very good fighter. I knew I was lucky to have beaten him twice, but it would've never happened without Theo's guidance.

"I'm gonna go shower if you guys don't mind waiting." I hesitated, giving them a moment.

"Nope go ahead."

"Yeah, go on. Maybe Adelaide and I can work on climbing this wall." Winston pointed at the rock wall.

"You think I can climb that?" Adelaide gasped.

"Sure you can. Race you?"

"Oh, you're on."

I shook my head and left the two of them to their race.

Jee was in the kitchen as I passed from the training room heading for the stairs. His eyes watched my movements, like each step I took was calculated and he needed to figure out why.

He seemed to be as wary of me as I was of him.

I headed up the stairs and took my shower. This day felt much the same as yesterday and it was mildly annoying, but I didn't feel right to complain because we were training, and leaving this place wasn't safe.

I hated being cooped up, staying in the manor all the time had nearly killed me, but I understood our safety was important.

Better to be stuck in here than dead.

Plus, I would be able to leave these walls eventually.

To breathe fresh air.

To practice magic.

I changed into a pair of sweatpants and a t-shirt. It was simple, but I really didn't care what I looked like. Twisting my hair into a knot, I secured it with an elastic. Dark circles surrounded my eyes when I gazed into the mirror above the dresser in the room I shared with Adelaide. I was sleeping okay, but it was restless. Lots of tossing and turning. I was surprised Adelaide hadn't kicked me onto the floor yet.

I didn't know how it was possible, but I thought I looked older somehow.

It was in my eyes. The hazel color reflected the sadness of someone who'd seen too much, lost too much, at their age.

Everything great in my life seemed to be slowly ripped away from me.

It made me fear the safety of Adelaide, Winston, and even Ethan.

Maybe my love was a curse, some sort of plague, wiping people out.

I wondered if I was meant to be alone, wandering aimlessly. The thought wasn't appealing. I didn't have many friends, never had, but I loved them with my whole heart. Having no one, I was sure the emptiness would suffocate me.

My heart already had an irreparable hole where Theo had been.

My dad too.

"You okay?"

I jumped at the sound of Adelaide's voice.

"Fine," I replied.

Fine.

What an ambiguous word.

Was anyone every really *fine* when they used that word?

I certainly wasn't.

"You looked like you were lost in thought." She closed the door behind her.

"Yeah, I ... uh ... was thinking."

"About what?" She dropped her towel and I turned away.

Adelaide didn't really care about privacy, but I did.

"It's not important."

She made a noise like she didn't believe me. "Jee ordered pizza," she changed the subject. "I hope you're hungry."

I opened my mouth to say *no I'm not*, but my stomach came to a sudden and roaring life at the mention of pizza.

"Starving."

"I'm decent," she said, and I turned around to find her dressed in similar apparel, her towel clutched in her arms.

"Who won?" I asked.

She snorted. "Not me. I have weak little bird arms." She pretended to flex her left arm and frowned at the weak muscle definition.

"You'll get there."

I knew she would, too, especially if she set her mind to it. Adelaide was a tough cookie.

"Enough chit-chat, food's waiting," she sing-songed as she swung the door open.

She danced down the hall to return her towel to the bathroom. I trudged behind her, shaking my head.

I wished I could be half as happy and carefree as she was.

Still, I knew she hurt.

I knew it in the way sometimes her shoulders would suddenly sag, or a crease would appear between her brow. She was just better at pretending than I was.

Then again, Theo was her brother, and he was my ...

My protector?

My love?

He was so much more than those things.

He was *everything*.

He was the sun, and the moon, and every star in the sky.

He was a million tiny, teal fireflies flying overhead.

He was snuck glances and wishful touches.

He was intense kisses and sharp words.

And he was gone.

When we reached the downstairs, the guys were sitting around on the couch, paper plates in hand, with a greasy pizza.

The scene was normal, average, nothing extraordinary, but still *nothing* was normal.

Nothing had been since the day Theo crashed into me—literally.

My whole life had been upended and I'd thought I was prepared for it, but I couldn't have been more wrong.

You couldn't prepare for something like this.

For magic, and violence, and so much upheaval.

"Grab a slice and stop staring," Jee scolded, not even looking at me.

I didn't know how he knew so much, just that he did.

Maybe he had eyes in the back of his head or something. I wouldn't be surprised.

I flipped the lid of the pizza box open on the coffee table and grabbed a slice.

I settled into the chair and Jee glared at me. "Don't get sauce or your greasy fingers on my furniture."

"Do you enjoy badgering people all the time?" I questioned with a raised brow, bringing the pizza to my mouth.

Adelaide sat on the floor, her legs tucked under the coffee table, eating her piece.

Jee tilted his head, thinking seriously about my question. "I'm sorry," he apologized, which surprised me. "I never thought of it like I was being rude, but I *am*. I'm ... I'm used to living on my own. Not even with Ethan, not for long at least, so having this many people here, in my space, is hard for me."

Now it was my turn to apologize. "I'm sorry too. I never thought of it like that."

Ethan had told us Jee lived alone, that he was paranoid, but I brushed it off.

It made sense, though, that Jee would be as uneasy having us here as we were being here.

We exchanged a small smile, and for a moment I believed, hoped at least, that everything would be okay.

chapter eight

I STARED OUT THE WINDOW, WATCHING the snowflakes swirl through the air before falling gracefully to the ground.

January had bled into February and now it was the start of March.

In Minnesota, though, you could hardly tell spring was around the corner. It looked ages away.

Today was supposed to be the first day we ventured out to practice our magic, Ethan and Jee having *finally* determined we were as safe as we could be, but it felt like the snow was trying to confine us in here. To these bare gray walls. The snow fell faster, the flakes larger— there already had to be a few fresh inches, not to mention the leftover sludge from the previous snowfall.

In the last month, my muscles had bulked up immensely. I wasn't anywhere near what Theo had been, or even Ethan, and I never would be, but for my small petite body I'd take it.

Fighting came easy for me. It was as natural as breathing, and I'd come to crave all our training sessions. In some ways, I was better than Ethan, but in others he was. We both learned from each other, and I liked that. It kept things from becoming stale.

I felt like I'd grown up a lot too since coming here—almost as if I'd aged a few years in a matter of weeks. In a way, I'd had to do a lot of growing up.

"You ready to go?" I jumped at the sound of Winston's voice.

I turned away from the window, wrapping my arms around myself.

"We're going? I thought the snow would stop us?"

He shook his head. "No, Ethan said he put a charm on it, sorta like they had at the school, to keep the snow from the area we'll be in. He said it won't be warm, but no snow is better than snow."

I looked down at my loose sweater falling off my shoulder and pair of plain black leggings.

Ethan and Jee had been forced to go shopping for the three of us since it wasn't right for him to keep conjuring stuff.

"I better change," I mumbled.

Winston watched me carefully, studying every movement I made.

I wanted to call him on it, to lash out with words, but I knew he wasn't my enemy. I'd been worse to him than he had to me. I'd *hurt* him and he'd always been nothing but kind. He was probably worried about me. I supposed I was doing a little better, but I still hurt. Theo's loss had me feeling off balance, like I'd lost a foot or something vital. My body yearned and ached for him in a way that wasn't normal grief.

Passing Winston, my shoulder bumped his slightly on accident. He stared after me as I jogged up the steps faster than normal.

The apartment was quiet, Jee was painting the last I saw, and Ethan and Adelaide must've been in the garage already—leaving Winston to fetch me.

I closed the bedroom door behind me and it latched with a quiet *ting*.

Adelaide and I had made ourselves at home, having to clasp onto some sort of normalcy, so I rifled through the dresser drawer for a pair of fighting leather and a long sleeve black shirt, then plucked a pair of boots from the closet.

It didn't take me long to change and then I was dashing back downstairs.

Winston waited at the bottom of the stairs, shoving his sandy brown hair from his eyes. It had grown longer and even shaggier in the last month. It was in desperate need of a trim, but the look sort of suited him.

He clucked his tongue when he saw me. "We can't have this."

I narrowed my eyes at him and glanced down at my outfit.

"What's wrong with it?"

"Nothing, but it's missing something."

He headed down the hall and opened a closet. He pulled out a thick piece of black fabric and handed it to me.

"What is it?" I asked stupidly. "A blanket?"

He laughed and shook his head. "No, silly, a cloak. Every good enchanter needs a cloak."

"A cloak," I whispered in surprise, unfolding the fabric.

I slung it around my shoulders and tied it in the front. It was long, drifting behind me on the ground like a train on a wedding dress. I brought the hood up and looked at Winston.

"How do I look?"

He smiled, his crooked teeth showing. "Like a bad ass."

I felt like a bad ass but I didn't say it out loud.

"We better go before they ditch us," he said, grabbing my hand to pull me toward the elevator.

I pulled my hand from his and he glanced at me.

"I-I'm sorry," I muttered, clasping my hands in front of me.

"It's okay," he said, but his eyes said it wasn't. "I didn't mean anything by it."

"I know." And I did, but it still felt weird.

His hand wasn't the one I wanted to feel.

I closed my eyes, and if I thought hard enough I could picture Theo standing in front of me, arms crossed over his chest, black t-shirt pulled taut. His dark brows scrunched together, black curls falling into his eyes, and that perpetual scowl I hated but had come to love.

Ding.

The elevator lift stopped in front of us and we stepped on, Winston closing the doors behind us.

We stood silently as it moved down to the garage and as we stepped off, a black vehicle blinked its lights at us, scaring me.

When my eyes adjusted to the dark nature of the garage I saw Ethan in the driver's seat and Adelaide beside him.

Winston and I climbed into the back of the all-black Range Rover—a vehicle I actually recognized since Dani's mom had one.

Dani.

I hadn't thought of her in months, too wrapped up in my strange new world, but an ache filled my chest all the same.

I missed her, and worried about her too. I was fearful something would happen to her because of me and it was the last thing I ever wanted.

"Whose car is this?" I asked, snapping my seatbelt into place.

"Jee's," Ethan answered, glancing in the rearview mirror at us.

"What happened to the other one? The one we came in?"

He backed out of the parking space and drove toward the exit. "Jee and I took it to a junkyard and had it crushed," he explained.

"Whoa, that seems kind of ... drastic."

He chuckled, turning right out of the garage. "We couldn't be sure whether the car was traceable, so we figured it was better to get rid of it."

"Oh, makes sense."

I glanced out the window at the city streets. People strolled along in heavy coats with cups of coffee in their hands. It all looked so simple and easy.

I missed being human—though I was never actually that. I supposed more than anything I missed the naivety of not knowing a whole other world existed alongside it. Things were simpler.

Now, my life was a whole big question mark with some purpose I had no idea how I was supposed to fulfill since I didn't even know what it was.

Eight months ago, I'd known where my life was going.

Sure, it was simple, and not exciting, but at least I'd *known*.

Now, I had no safe place, no Theo, and no clue what came next.

The uncertainty was stifling.

I felt Winston watching me, but I didn't turn from the window. He was worried about me, it was obvious, but I was *okay*.

Was I great? No, certainly not, but I was dealing and that had to count for something.

"How far away is this place?" I asked Ethan.

"About an hour out of the city. We didn't want to find any place close to the apartment in case we draw them in. Which we *shouldn't*, since I charmed the place we're going, but you never know."

"Are there … other things we could draw in? Besides the Iniquitous?" I shuddered as I remembered the Grindor that had been in my house when Theo had come for me. The creature had been the stuff of nightmares.

Ethan shrugged. "Yes, there's always the chance."

"What else is out there? What should we worry about, I mean."

"There are all sorts of monsters and creatures in this world, Mara. Too many to name."

I bit the inside of my cheek.

I hated not knowing what might be out there.

He glanced at me in the rearview mirror and sighed. "There are these things called seekers, and they do exactly that. The Iniquitous breed them like dogs and set them loose to find what they're searching for. Their job is to find whatever they're looking for and bring it back."

"Sounds ... lovely. What do they look like?"

"They're wolf-like, but larger, and more skeletal. They have no hair, only skin, and they're blind. They can smell what they're searching for from hundreds of miles away, though."

"Gross," Adelaide gagged. "I hope I never see one of those."

"If I have anything to say about it, you never will."

***

Ethan turned down a narrow path that really didn't even look like it was meant to be a road. Tree branches nearly scraped the sides of the car, and I feared Jee would lose his mind if we returned his car with a scratch or ding.

Ethan slammed on the brakes suddenly, the trees closing in on us.

"We have to walk from here."

He unbuckled his seatbelt and we followed suit.

He went around back and opened the trunk, pulling a black duffel bag from its depths. It looked heavy, and I immediately wondered what was in it, but I didn't ask.

"This way."

He started around the car and kept walking straight into the woods.

It was cold and windy, so I gathered the hood of my cloak onto my head and held it close around my body.

Adelaide, Winston, and I walked side by side. I'm sure we looked like a force to be reckoned with, both of them wearing cloaks as well.

Winston's was a deep midnight blue, almost black like mine, but Adelaide's was a bright crimson red and I couldn't help but be reminded of Little Red Riding Hood.

In front of us, Ethan's was black like mine, but designed differently. It was shorter and fit him more like a jacket than a cloak.

We trudged through the woods, our footprints leaving impressions in the snow.

"How far is it?" Adelaide asked. "We've been walking forever."

"We've been walking ten minutes," Winston scoffed.

"Exactly, *forever*," she intoned.

He sighed and shook his head, muttering under his breath.

"About a mile," Ethan answered.

"A *mile*," Adelaide shrieked. "Are you trying to kill us?"

"I know you're not out of shape," Winston mumbled.

She shot a glare at him. "No one asked you, Churchill."

She winced and swallowed thickly, her face growing shadowed with sadness. Her gaze drifted to the ground and she stumbled.

I grabbed her arm. "Are you okay?"

"Fine," she whispered, and I released her.

She picked up her speed and moved up to Ethan's side to walk with him.

Winston moved closer to me, our arms brushing as we walked.

"I know I haven't said much, but I am sorry, you know. I know you loved him, and I'm sorry you're hurting, both of you. He wasn't my favorite person, but I didn't hate him. I saw the …" he paused, gathering a breath. "I saw the way he looked at you, and there's no denying the way he felt about you. If I'm being completely honest I saw it from the beginning, the way you guys looked at each other, and I knew there was no competing with that, but I tried anyway."

I glanced up at him. He was slightly gangly and awkward, but he was cute, and he was my friend.

"There's a girl out there for you, Winston. I'm sorry it wasn't me."

He cracked a small smile. "You're an incredible girl, Mara, and you're going to do great things. I'm glad I at least get to witness it as your friend."

I forced a smile back at him. "Thanks."

Everybody kept telling me I was going to do great things, but I didn't believe them.

I was average and, if I was honest, I was scared.

How could someone so scared possibly do anything worthwhile?

Yes, I wanted to fight back, I wanted to end this, but that was because I was angry at what I'd lost, at what the Iniquitous kept taking not from me but all of us, and I didn't think that made me brave. Maybe a little stupid, but definitely not brave.

"I'm lucky to have you as a friend," I told him honestly. "I don't deserve you."

I really didn't, not after the way I'd used him. In the beginning I hadn't meant to, but when it became obvious I couldn't overcome my feelings for Theo I let it drag on because Winston was safe, and simple, and I hoped maybe he'd get under Theo's skin.

"I know you think you don't, but you do. You're not a bad person."

"Thanks." I looped my arm through his and rested my head on his shoulder as we strolled behind the others.

His words were kind, but I didn't really believe them.

There was so much I hadn't done right, and leaving Theo behind was one of the worst.

I knew it was what I was *supposed* to do, what *he* wanted me to do, but that didn't make it right.

He was more than my protector, he was my other half, and we should've fought side by side, back to back, if that's what it took.

If he went down then so did I, because without him my heartbeat was the saddest song. It was empty, an echo of what it once was.

"Not much longer," Ethan called back.

"Do you think we're safe here?" I whispered to Winston, low enough there was no chance Ethan heard. "Can we trust Jee?"

Winston grew quiet and when I looked up at him I could see his lips twisting as he thought.

Jee had been less harsh lately, but there was something about him that still unnerved me. He saw too much, knew too much, and I guess as a seer that was the point, but it didn't make me feel any better.

"I think we can," he finally replied. "He's different, that's for sure, but I don't think he'd betray us. I think he's more afraid of *us* betraying him. A seer would be a hot commodity for the Iniquitous if they got their hands on him. I'm sure he's afraid. I would be."

I sighed and straightened up, letting go of his arm.

"I hate the fact we always have to look over our shoulder now, live in fear, nothing is easy or simple anymore and it's not fair."

"Nothing's fair, Mara, that's the way of the world." He shoved his hands into the pockets of his cloak, the wind billowing it behind him.

He was right. Nothing was fair. The world liked to chew you up and spit you back up. It liked to test you, to see how far it could push you before you broke.

I refused to break.

It wasn't long before we stepped through the shimmery orb Ethan had erected previously around the spot he'd found.

Inside, there was no snow but, like he'd warned, it was chilly.

Thankfully, I was warm from our trek through the woods, and I was sure the spell practicing would keep me that way.

"I'll work with Adelaide," Ethan announced. "Winston, you can take Mara."

I glanced at Winston and he chuckled softly. I wasn't sure if it was a good thing or a bad thing he'd partnered me with Winston.

I had a feeling Winston wasn't going to go easy on me. Again, I found myself thankful for the extra training Theo had done with me. Without it I'd be feeling like a lost puppy.

The clearing was large enough the four of us could spread out to practice and not be close to each other, in case a spell went awry.

"Where should we start?" I asked Winston.

He shrugged and took off his cloak, rolling up the sleeves of his flannel, so I did the same.

"Have you worked on offensive spells any?" he asked, squinting from the sunlight shining through the tree branches.

"Yeah, a little." I stood with my hands on my hips.

"Show me what you got." He gestured with a *bring it on* motion.

I paused. "Uh ... are you sure?"

"Mhmm," he murmured. "I can't help you if I don't know what I'm working with."

I nodded. "Okay."

I closed my eyes and let out a breath, rolling my shoulders to loosen up.

Nerves coursed through my veins. I didn't want to make a fool of myself. It felt like it'd been ages since I'd last practiced with Theo.

I tapped into the power that always seemed to hum in my core. It buzzed to life, vibrating through my body and out through my limbs.

I felt the warm lick of flames and opened my eyes, throwing a burst at Winston.

"Whoa," he cried, knocking it away with a shield. He still stumbled a few feet back from the force.

He looked at me with shock and I shrugged.

"I like fire," I mumbled.

Fire was one of the easiest things for me to conjure. I noticed I was easily able to tap into the elements, earth, fire, water, and air. Fire spoke to me the most.

"I think you've mastered fire. We can cross it off the list."

I snapped my thumb against my middle finger and a fire ignited on my fingers. "Yeah, I think so." I grinned and closed my fist, extinguishing the flame.

He chuckled. "What else you got?"

My smile grew wider.

I closed my eyes, imagining the air swirling around me, blowing the leaves in circles, and creating a vortex

When I opened my eyes I saw nothing but leaves. I was completely enclosed in them.

I calmed myself and the wind slowed, the leaves settling on the ground.

Winston stood across from me, his hair mused.

"What do you need me for?" he joked.

I laughed. "Lots of things, I'm sure." Though I *wanted* to be great at everything right off the bat. The idea of failing again and again didn't sit well with me.

Ethan walked over to us and handed Winston the duffel bag he'd brought.

"There's some stuff in here you might want to check out."

He headed back to Adelaide, and Winston knelt on the ground, rifling through it.

Eventually he pulled out a teacup and a kettle.

He opened the kettle and waved his hand over it. Steam began to billow out of the inside.

He set them both on the ground and sat down.

I did the same sitting across from him with the cup and kettle between us.

"Pour it into the cup."

I smirked. "Oh, that's easy."

After learning to conjure a specific book off a shelf, I knew this would be a piece of cake.

I stared at the kettle, visualizing in my mind what I wanted it to do.

It began to shake, and tip forward. I urged it on, to lift and pour.

The top of the kettle shot off, flying into the air and disappearing, and the hot tea came spewing out straight up into the air.

Winston and I both jumped up and scuttled back so we'd be out of the way when it rained down.

As the hot tea trickled down onto the ground I frowned.

"That was *not* what I planned."

He chuckled. "That's why we have to practice."

I crinkled my nose. I was disappointed, I wanted it to be easy. Well, not *easy*. I wanted to believe I was *worthy*. If I sucked at this whole enchanter thing how could I possibly be chosen?

Winston chuckled and collected the top from the kettle. "Let's try again. Take it slow."

He filled the kettle back up and I sat down.

"Close your eyes," he whispered softly, his voice soothing. "Visualize what you want."

I straightened my shoulders and behind my closed eyelids I pictured what I wanted.

D-Don't o-over

My eyes popped open. "Theo," I whispered.

"Huh?" Winston looked at me questioningly.

M-Mara n-no

"Theo!" I shouted and stood up.

Ethan and Adelaide stopped what they were doing, running over.

I spun in circles shouting his name. "Theo! Theo answer me! *Theodore!*"

S-Stop

I covered my ears with my hands and sunk to my knees. My head throbbed, but I pushed away the pain.

Theo please, is that you? I begged brokenly in the confines of my mind.

THEO!

My shout echoed against a void.

The voice was gone, if it'd even really been there to start with. Was it possible I was losing my mind? Slowly being driven mad by the loss of my protector?

Three sets of eyes looked at me questioningly.

I broke down sobbing.

"He's gone," I cried, wrapping my arms around my body, trying to hold in the broken pieces of my heart. "He always leaves."

They looked at me pityingly and I cried harder.

I didn't understand what the voice was, whether it was real, his ghost maybe, or a figment of my imagination.

Whatever it was, it was too much to bear.

chapter nine

I BRUSHED MY DAMP HAIR, staring out the bedroom window as more snow fell from the sky. I heard Adelaide's feet pad across the floor and the bed squeak as she knelt on it.

My breaths were quiet and even, and I focused on those instead of the feel of her eyes on me.

Avoidance had been my middle name since we got back from practicing.

I couldn't bring myself to speak to any of them about what happened, though I knew they were all curious. I didn't understand what'd happened, so how could I expect them to?

Adelaide sighed from the bed. "Will you at least look at me?"

I lowered the brush and turned to look at her from the windowsill. There wasn't much space, my butt barely fit, but I didn't care.

"What happened out there today?" Her dark blue eyes were full of concern and that only made me feel worse.

I shrugged.

"Mara," she huffed, and rolled her eyes.

She glanced down at the bed, toying with a loose thread in the quilt. "You screamed his name, Mara. Did you hear him?"

Silence.

"Dammit, Mara. He's *my* brother. I deserve to know if he's alive. If he's hurting." For once, I saw anger flash in her eyes. Adelaide rarely lost her temper, she had her shit together better than the rest of us, but I was currently pushing all of her buttons. I couldn't blame her for snapping.

I shook my head. "Ade ..." I paused, not knowing how to continue. "It's just a ghost, a memory, that's all."

She ground her teeth together. "Do you really believe that?"

I swallowed thickly. "I have to. I ... I saw him *die*. I can't give myself false hope only to lose him all over again. It'll kill me. I hurt all the time already. I don't want to hurt worse."

Sadness filled her eyes. "You're right." She bit her lip, fighting back tears. She'd been hopeful after my outburst and I hated breaking her heart, but the voice was probably a figment of my imagination. Conjured by my desire for him to be alive.

"I miss him so much," I confessed, "I think my brain is conjuring his voice so it's like he never left. Or maybe it's his ghost trying to guide me. I don't know," I rambled. "But I don't think he's alive. The voice ... it's not normal. It's faint. Like ... like he's somewhere *else*, beyond, and trying to break through."

"You'll tell me if anything changes, right? If you think he's alive?"

I felt the firefly in my necklace flutter.

"You know I will."

Her eyes held hope and for that I felt awful.

Hope was the most crushing emotion to exist on the planet.

***

"Cheer up, buttercup, you look like someone pissed in your Cheerios. That's *not* piss, right?" Jee pointed to my bowl of cereal.

"No," I replied glumly.

Hearing Theo's voice yesterday had put me in a funk, and I wasn't sure I was ready to step back into the ring, so to speak.

But Ethan was demanding after breakfast we all head to the woods to practice more.

It's all I'd wanted for months, but now I was desperate to take it back.

He slid into the stool beside me. "What's wrong?"

"Why do you care?" I stirred my cereal around the bowl. I wasn't even hungry. I was never hungry anymore.

He chuckled. "I don't if I'm being honest. I thought ..." He lowered his voice and leaned in. "You might like to talk to someone who isn't quite as ... invested."

I glanced around us. Adelaide and Winston were arguing over the TV while they ate their breakfast and Ethan was upstairs.

"I've heard his voice in my head twice. Theo's," I whispered. "The first time was shortly after we got here. We were in your training room. I heard him tell me to duck. Then yesterday, I heard him when we were practicing magic. Both times it was like he was speaking to me from way far away. Quiet, kind of gravelly. Like static. I know I have to be imagining it, or maybe it's his ghost, I don't know. It scares me he might be alive, out there somewhere, trapped, and I'm not doing anything about it. But I *saw* the sword go into him. I saw him *die*. And I hate feeling this false sense of hope. I want to squash it so I'm not disappointed."

Jee picked up his cup of coffee and took a sip. His eyes were thoughtful, pondering over what I'd said.

"You know it's possible it is his ghost."

"You don't think I'm crazy?"

He shook his head. "When you have a protector, and a bond like you two have, it's not a stretch to think even death can't break it."

"What do I do? Can I speak to him? Can I ..." I tilted my head to his ear and whispered, "Can I bring him back?"

He got a faraway look. "The dead are better left that way. That kind of magic ... Even the Iniquitous would be out of their minds to try something like that."

I wrung my fingers together. "Do you know who my dad is?"

He nodded, looking toward the cabinets across from us. "Thaddeus," he whispered. "I knew him once upon a time. Scary guy. Powerful, conniving, and ... brilliant."

"You knew him?" I whispered.

He grinned, his smile almost predatory like a shark. "I'm not all enchanter, dear girl."

I gulped. "What are you?" The hairs on the back of my neck stood on end.

Ethan clomped down the steps. "I want you three in the car in ten minutes."

Jee tilted his head at me. "A story for another day."

He slipped away and disappeared who knew where.

His easel had vanished from the living space a few days after we got here. I didn't know where he'd hid it. I hadn't found an extra room, but it didn't mean anything, because *magic*.

I dumped my cereal and went upstairs to throw some clothes on and put my hair back in a sloppy ponytail.

The last thing I wanted to do today was this.

I couldn't back out, though, not when I'd pushed for this.

Mostly, I was terrified of hearing Theo's voice again—actually, it scared me more that I might *not* hear it.

Yesterday had been the first time in months I'd heard him.

I'd chalked the first time up to my imagination, but I was having a harder time letting go of yesterday. I'd *heard* him. I knew I had.

But was it *him?* Or my imagination playing the cruelest of tricks on me?

***

"Okay, I'm calling it a day," Ethan announced.

I slumped onto the ground, exhausted. I was drained from using my magic.

Winston said the more I used it the stronger I'd get and the less draining it would be when we worked on spells. I was disappointed, though, since Theo and I had worked so hard before that I wasn't stronger than I was. But I had to remind myself, I'd only come into my powers less than a year ago.

More than anything I was saddened I hadn't heard Theo today.

Again, I began to doubt myself, to question whether or not it was my imagination.

Winston's boots appeared in my field of vision and I lifted my head from the ground.

"You okay?" he asked, and I nodded. "You did good today."

I huffed out a laugh.

"No, seriously, you did."

"Thanks," I muttered.

"You're being too hard on yourself, you're incredible. You got the summoning spell on the second try. Do you have any idea how long it took me to learn that one?"

I shook my head.

"Months." He crouched down beside me. "I know you want to master everything in the blink of an eye but that's not realistic."

"You're right," I admitted, "but I still wish otherwise."

He chuckled. "Don't we always."

Standing up straight he held out his hand to me and I took it.

"Thanks for working with me."

He smiled. "You don't need to thank me."

"Yes, I do."

Ethan clapped his hands together, calling our attention.

"I thought we could stop at a restaurant on the way back and get something to eat."

"Really?" Adelaide beamed. "That'd be so nice."

I nodded in agreement. It was hard being stuck in Jee's apartment all the time. Getting out some was nice.

"We better start back to the car then."

Adelaide looped her arm through mine, and the guys walked ahead of us. Winston kept looking back at us questioningly and I smiled to assure him I was okay.

"Did you hear him today?" she whispered.

"Adelaide," I breathed. "Please, don't go there."

"It's only a question," she mumbled.

I sighed, knowing I wasn't getting out of this. "No, I didn't hear him."

"You're lying," she growled.

I shook my head. "I wish I was."

Tears pooled in her eyes. "It isn't fair."

"Nothing's fair." Trudging through the thick leaves, sticks, and clumps of snow that had begun to melt, I added, "We can't get hung up on the unfairness. If we do we'll drive ourselves insane."

"I want someone to tell me it was a bad dream," she confessed. "I want to wake up and for it to all go away."

"Me too."

I felt like I was missing half of myself, and I didn't think I'd ever recover from it. I'd have to learn to live in a new way.

"Do you think he's watching over us?" Her voice was soft. "Wherever he is?"

A snowflake swirled through the air and I answered without hesitation.

"Yes."

***

We stopped at a local Italian restaurant. It was small, family-owned, with pictures of generations of owners and their families on the walls.

I swirled my pasta around and took a bite. Winston and Ethan joked about something and Adelaide sat sadly beside me.

She'd been down since our conversation in the woods. I didn't know how to make it better, but I couldn't lie to her and tell her I heard him when I didn't. Giving her false hope wouldn't be good, especially when the voice probably didn't even exist.

Adelaide pushed her food around her plate, much like I'd done with my cereal this morning.

I hated seeing her like this. I missed the happy, sweet, bubbly person she'd been when I first met her. The person who'd been willing to defy orders to be my friend.

"Hey." I knocked my shoulder against hers and she looked at me. "I don't like seeing you like this."

She frowned and exhaled a heavy breath. "Today's ... a bad day. Some days hurt more, you know?"

I knew exactly what she meant. "I know. You can talk to me. Only if you want."

"Thanks." She gave me a small smile.

I doubted she would, but I wanted her to have the option. I knew how I was, though, and I preferred to keep everything bottled inside. It wasn't easy talking about your feelings—your hopes and fears.

Winston snagged a breadstick from the basket. "Come on, smile!" He pointed the breadstick at Adelaide and then me. "We're out, we're eating good food, and we're with friends."

I pressed my fingers to the corners of my lips and forced a smile. "Look at me, I'm smiling."

He tossed a napkin, at me and I laughed, catching it before it landed on my shirt.

"That doesn't count and you know it, Pryce."

I threw the napkin back at him. "How about this?" This time I gave him a genuine smile—granted it was over exaggerated and cheesy but beggars couldn't be choosers.

"I'll accept that."

"Wise man," I laughed. I picked up my fork and swirled more pasta around it.

"Your turn." He turned his attention to Adelaide.

She rested her head in her hand and gave a small sad smile.

Winston frowned. "What's wrong?"

"I miss my brother, that's all." She shrugged like it was no big deal.

Winston swallowed. "It's okay to miss him."

"I know, but missing him is hard. If I miss him it means he's really gone. I know it's been months, but I'm not ready to accept it."

With only a few words she broke my heart.

I'd been so caught up with how I felt with his loss, I hadn't stopped to think about her.

Of course, I knew she was hurting, he was her brother after all, but she'd kept herself more together than I had so somewhere along the way I started thinking she was okay with it.

But she'd lost her parents, and now him—she had no one left.

It wasn't something you accepted over night.

Loss also had a way of sneaking up on you when you least expected it. You'd think you were doing fine, and then out of nowhere something would remind you of the person and you'd feel the loss all over again.

Winston reached across the table and placed his hand over hers. She looked up at him and they exchanged something in their glance before he cleared his throat and sat back.

"How are you guys doing with the training?" Winston asked Ethan.

Even though we were in the same field training, we didn't really pay much attention to what Adelaide and Ethan were up to.

"She's doing well." Ethan smiled at her across the table. "I'm sure in a month's time she'll be exceptional."

Adelaide's cheeks heated with his praise. "Thank you," she mumbled awkwardly.

I bumped her shoulder with mine. "Own it, rock star."

She shook her head, unwilling to bask in the praise.

We finished eating and headed out and back to the car.

I lingered on the street a moment longer, letting the others get into the parked car. I looked up at the sky, at the sun shining between the foggy clouds.

"If you're there," I whispered, "if you're listening, know I love you, and I'm so, so, sorry."

The words didn't feel good enough, but they were all I had.

chapter ten

I DID EVERYTHING YOU WANTED," *a shaky voice pleaded.*

"Not everything." *The second voice I recognized instantly.*

Thaddeus.

"She got away. It wasn't my fault. I did everything—"

"Shut up, Finnley!"

Finnley? As in Finn?

"You were supposed to bring her to me and you didn't! You failed your duty, you failed yourself, and most importantly, you failed me."

My body glided through the shadows into the room. Moonlight shone through a window, lighting up the hunched figure on the floor.

Finn was a ghost of the man I knew. Gone was his handsomeness and boyish smile. He looked like he'd aged twenty years. He was too thin, and his face sagged, his eyes wrinkled around the corners.

"Failure is not an option," Thaddeus continued to a kneeling Finn.

"I know, sir, but—"

"I don't want to hear you grovel. Groveling is for weak, pathetic men. Is that you?"

"N-No, sir."

"I trusted you to get the job done and you didn't. I'm not in the habit of giving second chances—"

"Please, sir—"

"Shut up!" Thaddeus bellowed. "And listen to me. I'm giving you one more chance, but if you fail me you know what happens." Thaddeus grazed his fingers over a sword hilt strapped to his side. "Prove to me you're worth it."

"I will, sir. I'll do anything. Anything."

Thaddeus grazed his fingers over Finn's forehead. "I always wanted a son."

"I'll be your son. I'll be—"

Thaddeus pulled his sword out in one swift movement and it arced through the air, right through Finn's neck.

Finn's face showed pure astonishment before his neck dropped from his body and rolled to the ground.

Blood spurting from the stump left behind. The floor quickly turned scarlet.

"Are you watching, little one? I feel you there."

He turned in a circle, surveying the room. His eyes landed on a spot on the wall and he spoke to it as if it was me. I breathed a sigh of relief that he didn't actually know I was there.

"I thrive on the vulnerability, the begging, the pleading. It brings me joy to hold someone's life in my hands, knowing I can sever their tie to Earth at any moment. Do you like it too?"

He clucked his tongue.

"Did you know you had a brother?"

I gasped softly and his gaze swiveled, settling close to where I stood.

Well, actually, I wasn't standing. I wasn't there. But I could see.

"He died before you were born. He was sick, and I wanted to save him. I wanted to do whatever it took to give my son his life, and it turned me into this." He pounded a fist against his chest. "Monsters aren't born, Mara. Monsters are made."

He paced the length of the room, his boots tracking the bright red blood oozing from Finn's body, but he didn't seem to care.

"Then, when your mother discovered what I'd done to save your brother, she ran from me. From me. Her husband, her best friend, her partner. She abandoned me when I needed her most, but what I didn't know at

the time was she wasn't running to save herself. She was running to save you."

I gulped into the darkness, my heart pounding.

"She hid my child from me, because she was afraid I'd hurt you. I'd never hurt you, not my child. But you've got to stop running from me. We need to be a family again."

I wanted to speak out, to ask him what happened to my brother. Whether he was dead or alive. What his name was. Something. But I was terrified if I spoke he'd find me and this would no longer be a dream.

I'd be trapped.

"Come to me, little one, because if you don't ..." he paused, clasping his hands behind his back as he stared out the window at the night sky. "You'll lose everything you hold dear. I promise you that."

***

I jolted awake with a scream, my body drenched in sweat.

Shoving my hair out of my eyes I looked beside me at Adelaide. She sat up, looking at me with questioning eyes. I could tell I'd frightened her, and she was probably still half asleep.

The door to our room burst open and on reflex I grabbed the dagger I kept hidden under my pillow, but it was only Winston and Theo.

No, not Theo.

Ethan.

I hated that for a split second my imagination had played tricks on me.

"What's going on?" Ethan asked stiffly, surveying the room.

"Are you okay?" whispered Adelaide, touching her fingers softly to my arm.

I winced and she quickly retracted her hand. My skin was overly sensitive and her touch had felt like a thousand tiny needles searing me.

"I-It was a dream," I stuttered. With a shake of my head I corrected, "A vision."

"A vision?" Winston repeated. "Are you like Jee?"

"No, no, it's not like that." I shook my head. "It's more like I see things as they're happening, and it's always with my ... with Thaddeus. It's like I'm connected to him in some way."

"Connected?" Winston repeated. "How is that possible?" He looked at Ethan for answers.

Ethan shrugged. "She is his daughter. Anything is possible, I suppose. It could be a spell, or it could be because he's chosen, her mother is, and so is she."

"Do Chosen Ones not always have children who are chosen as well?"

"It's very rare," he admitted. "There hasn't been one such as you, born of *two*, very powerful Chosen Ones, in hundreds of years."

"So your parents aren't chosen?" I asked Winston.

He shook his head. "No, they're perfectly normal."

"Chosen Ones are selected by ... well, no one really knows, but something out there decides who is and why. That's why it's rare for Chosen Ones to also have chosen children. It's not in your DNA it's ... given to you."

I thought back to the manor and Jessamine who'd had chosen parents but was a perfectly normal enchanter, but yet because of her heritage the Iniquitous would still like to get their hands on her.

"Do you think I'm in danger in these *dreams?* It's like he can sense me. He knows I'm there but he can't see me."

Ethan worried his bottom lip between his teeth. "I don't know," he admitted.

That didn't help me breathe any easier.

"What did you see in your dream?" he asked.

I swallowed thickly.

"It was Finn, he was talking to Finn. Finn said he did everything he asked, but Thaddeus said he didn't. He didn't get ... *me.*" I squeaked, the thought terrifying if they got their hands on me like they wanted. "It sounded like Thaddeus was going to give him another chance, but then Finn said ..." I paused, and decided to omit what I'd heard about a son and my possible brother. No one seemed to know about him and I thought it was better if I didn't spill the beans. "He said something to make him mad, and he killed him. He's dead."

Ethan's cheeks hollowed. "Blood hungry bastard," he muttered. "And I can't believe Finn, that back-stabbing asshole. He was my friend. I trusted him."

"I think he's how they got into the manor that night. Maybe even in New York too."

Ethan scrubbed a hand over his face. "Try to get some sleep. I need to talk to Jee."

"Hey, Ethan?" I hedged at the mention of Jee.

"Yeah?"

"Jee said he's not completely enchanter. What else is he?"

Ethan raised a brow. "He told you that?"

I nodded.

Ethan sighed, fighting a smile. "I'll let him tell you. Okay?" I nodded. "Night."

He slipped out of the room, Winston following with one last look over his shoulder at us as he closed the door.

"Are you okay?" Adelaide asked again.

For once, I didn't lie. "No."

I began to cry. Seeing Finn murdered brought back the haunting memories of watching them kill Theo.

She wrapped her arms around me and we cried together.

chapter eleven

YOU'VE BEEN AVOIDING ME." I slid into a chair next to Jee.

He looked up from a bowl of oatmeal. "Is it me or does this look like something not even an infant would eat?" He wrinkled his nose at the thick pale goo.

"Then why'd you make it?"

"Ethan told me I can't eat ice cream for breakfast every day. What's unacceptable about ice cream? Ice cream's never hurt anyone."

"I agree."

He raised a brow. "Why thank you." He threw his bowl into the sink and oatmeal splattered on the sides. "I'll clean it up later," he mumbled.

"I've been trying to talk to you all week but you keep disappearing." I rested my elbow on the counter and my head in my hand, feigning innocence.

He batted his eyes. "Me? Never." He pressed a hand to his chest, acting positively scandalized I'd suggest such a thing.

"Mhmm," I hummed.

He chuckled. "I know what you want."

"Do you?"

He nodded thoughtfully. "Just ask."

"What are you?"

"My mom's an enchanter, and my dad is a fairy." He shrugged like it was no big deal.

"How does that happen?" I blurted, shocked. That hadn't been the answer I was expecting. I don't know what exactly I *did* expect.

"Well, you see," he began. "My dad put his penis in—"

"Okay, okay, okay," I pleaded, holding my hands up for him to stop. "I get it."

He chuckled. "You asked."

"What do fairies even look like?"

He shrugged. "They're pale, but a funny pale not quite white, but sort of ashen. They have slightly pointed ears—it's not obvious so they can get by in the human world. It looks more like a birth defect than anything else."

"Do they fly?" I asked stupidly.

He shook his head and laughed under his breath. "Yes, but not like you're thinking. They don't sprout wings from their back and fly away. They … transform." He shrugged like his explanation was enough.

"Transform?" I questioned.

He cupped his hands and blew into them.

A tiny burst of light appeared and flew around us. It looked like a butterfly at first, small wings and body, but I quickly saw it was a person.

It disappeared with a pop, like a bubble.

"That's not a real one, of course, just an illusion, but that's what they look like."

"Amazing," I murmured, in complete awe.

I didn't know how I'd missed out on this world my whole life. I knew it was for my safety, but I still felt a sense of loss.

"Do you see them often?" I asked.

He shook his head. "No, and since my mom's growing older, it bothers me, but I know they're safe and that's what matters. I'll see them again one day."

"So, because you're half fae you'll live longer, right?"

He grinned. "Bet you wouldn't believe I'm almost fifty."

My jaw dropped. "That's how you knew my dad, isn't it?"

He nodded. "We grew up together."

"Wow. You don't look older than twenty-five at most."

He chuckled and his dark hair tumbled over his forehead. "There are some perks to this."

"Is that why you're a seer? Because of being half enchanter and half fae?"

"Let's just say, my mixed blood gives me abilities most would only dream of."

"Most?" I repeated.

He grinned, looking me over. "You've never figured out how special you are, have you?"

"N-No," I stuttered, taken aback and wondering what exactly he meant. "Tell me."

He shook his head. "I'm sorry, but it's not time."

"What does that mean?"

He shrugged. "It's not the right time," he repeated.

***

Sweat dripped from my body from the exertion of performing so many spells.

"Maraaaa."

I froze where I stood, my heart pounding. I held my breath, listening carefully for the voice.

"Mara?" Winston probed.

"Shh," I hushed him.

"Maara."

I slapped my hands over my ears. *"Theo, are you there? Can you hear me?"*

I squished my eyes closed, focusing on the echoing emptiness of my mind.

"I-I'm heeeere. I'm aaalways h-heeere."

I swallowed thickly, tears prickling my eyes. *"Are you really there? Or is this all in my head? Oh, Theo. I miss you so much."*

"I-I know. I f-feel you."

"You feel me?"

Silence stretched on, and finally. *"Y-Yes."*

"Does that mean ... are you alive?"

More silence.

I waited patiently.

Minutes passed, and I knew Winston was growing more confused.

The others watched on, curious as well.

"Theo? Are you still there? Theo?"

When he didn't reply, my heart clenched, but I reminded myself I'd heard him longer this time, and there was no way it'd been my imagination—I couldn't have made all of it up, right? He didn't answer my questions, but ...

I lowered my hands. "It's Theo. I-I hear him," I whispered. "I'm definitely hearing him. He spoke longer this time."

I knew in my gut he was there. I also knew it didn't mean he was alive, but it was more than I had before.

Somehow, someway, he existed.

Ethan stared shell-shocked at me. "Hearing voices isn't exactly good. Enchanters have gone crazy because of that."

Adelaide burst into tears, her sobs drowning out his words. "He must be alive."

I shook my head sadly. "I don't know. I asked him, but he was gone already."

I wanted to believe she was right, he was alive, but I couldn't be sure. He was my protector after all, and everyone always said we were special, so what if, even in death, we were still tethered together?

But Ethan's words lingered in my mind too.

Hearing voices isn't exactly good. Enchanters have gone crazy because of that.

What if it wasn't Theo at all—what if I *was* going crazy?

Or what if this was yet another ploy by Thaddeus?

chapter twelve

THE VOICE GREW STRONGER.

As March bled into April and April into May, I heard him more and more. The voice was so real I often sensed he was standing over my shoulder guiding me, helping me. At times I swore I felt the pressure of his hand on my shoulder but when I looked there was never anyone there.

Ethan watched me closely, I'm sure looking for any sign I was going downhill, but so far I hadn't had any side effects from hearing him. Maybe it was because he'd been my protector that things were different, but I didn't want to speculate too much because then I *would* go crazy.

I brought the hood of the cloak up over my head, blocking the chilly wind.

Even though it was May, Minnesota didn't know that. There'd been a light dusting of snow the night before.

I followed behind Ethan, Adelaide, and Winston hoping to hear Theo's voice.

I was worried I was becoming dependent on the sound of his voice. A desperate druggie needing their next fix. Hearing him made it feel like he was still here. Sometimes I could close my eyes and listen to him and it was like he'd never even gone.

It was probably why there was a real fear of me losing my mind. I could become obsessed with the voice in my head—with a life I could never have.

He'd never answer me when I asked if he was dead or alive—I figured it was because he didn't want to hurt me with the answer, but I hoped anyway.

The small chance that he was alive kept me going.

We came into the clearing and separated.

It wasn't long until I had to take off my cloak.

Winston and I had been working on defensive and offensive magic for a few weeks, and I was getting better and better. Most of the spells weren't easy, and weren't things I'd normally learn at my age, but the situation called for it.

I shot a burst of bright blue light at Winston and it knocked him back.

That's it, doll face.

I warmed at Theo's praise. *Thank you.*

"Good one," he chuckled. "I think you nearly broke my arm." He clutched his right arm.

"Sorry," I apologized sheepishly.

He shook it out and then shot a blazing mass of orange sparks at me.

I dropped down into a crouch and a bubble burst around me, blocking the spell.

He laughed and danced on the balls of his feet as I stood.

I cupped my hands and a purple orb appeared. I threw it at him and he threw out his arm to block it, but was unsuccessful. The orb hit him in the center of the chest and spread, wrapping around him entirely. It lifted him into the air and dropped him back to the ground before the purple shattered like glass and littered the ground. It disappeared in seconds.

Theo cackled in my mind, and I smirked.

Winston sat up slowly, his hair sticking up in every direction.

He rubbed his sore back. "Ugh, I think *you* need to be training me. What the hell was that?"

I shrugged. "I felt in my gut what to do."

A lot of times I just got this feeling deep inside my belly and somehow my mind knew what to do.

He shook his head and stood up, his back hunched. "That's going to hurt in the morning."

Good for you, Churchill.

I laughed, amused at the voice in my mind.

"What's so funny?" he asked.

"Nothing."

They knew I heard Theo, but it was a headache to constantly repeat everything he said. Besides, I didn't think Winston would appreciate this particular sentiment.

I felt a fluttering against my cheek and closed my eyes.

I wish I could touch you.

Was that you?

It was as much of me as I can give.

Theo … this isn't fair. I need you.

I'll find my way back to you.

How?

I don't know, but I will.

I love you.

Not as much as I love you.

My lower lip began to tremble. It was so unfair. I'd found the greatest love of my life, possibly of anyone's life, and had it ripped away.

It was such a cruel joke.

"Hey," whispered Winston. "What's wrong?"

I hadn't heard him move but he was suddenly in front of me, wiping a lone tear from my cheek. "I miss him, that's all."

He frowned. "I know, and I'm sorry."

"It's not fair," I whined. "I lost my mom before I even knew her, the only man I knew as my father, and now Theo. Am I destined to lose everyone I love?"

He shook his head. "I can't believe fate's cruel. Not for someone like you. You're *good*, and you deserve to be happy. But everything happens for a reason—fate has a plan, even if we can't see it at the time."

I nodded at his words. He was right, even if I didn't like it.

"I'm sorry, I'm sorry, I'm sorry!" we heard Adelaide chant, and we looked to find her running over to Ethan who was clutching his face.

We hurried over, worried Ethan was seriously hurt.

"Are you okay? Let me see." Adelaide tugged on his arm.

He let his hand fall away and I slapped a hand over my mouth to hold in my laughter.

"How bad is it?" he asked.

Adelaide snickered and Winston snorted.

"Um, well." She bit her lip. "You ... um..."

"Spit it out," he growled.

"You have no eyebrows, mate," Winston told him.

"Fuck." Ethan hung his head. "No more playing with fire for you."

Adelaide looked contrite. "I didn't mean to."

He shook his head. "I know you didn't, but I still have no eyebrows."

"Is there a spell to make them grow?" I asked, trying to be helpful.

"No," he growled. "I need a break."

He stalked off into the woods.

"I really made him mad, didn't I?" Adelaide asked no one in particular. "I didn't mean to. I was aiming for his chest."

"I think you need to work on your aim then." Winston chuckled. "Maybe we should get you some archery targets."

"Oh, shut up." She playfully swatted his chest and rolled her eyes.

They exchanged a look and I quickly turned away, feeling like I was spying on something I *so* should not be seeing.

I could see Adelaide and Winston as a couple, though. They balanced each other out. Winston was more quiet and laidback, while Adelaide was a hyper spaz who never shut up. They kind of *worked* in some strange way.

He better stay away from my sister.

I sighed. *Don't you want her to be happy?*

No.

Theo, I scolded. *He'd be good for her.*

You know what else is good for her? A chastity belt.

You're impossible.

It's part of my charm, and you love it.

Yeah, I guess I do.

Winston worked with the both of us, and by the time Ethan returned it was getting late so we headed back to Jee's.

Jee had already made dinner, which was rare, so he must've been in a particularly good mood.

We all sat around together in the living room.

I balanced my bowl of soup on my legs and cleared my throat.

"We've been practicing for months now, and I think we'll be ready to start pursuing the Iniquitous soon, but we also need to figure out who Cleo is."

"Cleo?" Jee repeated. "The old bat?"

"Um ..." I paused. "You know her?"

"I only know one Cleo, and she's ... interesting, to say the least."

I couldn't believe I hadn't said something sooner to Jee about Cleo. Up until the last few months, though, I hadn't really trusted him. There was still something about him that made me nervous, but he *was* different. Now that I knew he was half enchanter and half fae, it made more sense, the strange aura he put out.

"How do we find her?"

He chuckled. "Hold on to your weave—the mall."

"The mall?" I repeated.

"Yeah, she has this fortune teller stand in the mall."

"You've got to be kidding me. She's *here?* In *Minnesota?* At a *mall?*"

"That's what I said. Can you hear? Should you clean the wax out of your ears?"

I rolled my eyes. "I can't believe of all places, she's *here*."

"What can I say? All the freak enchanters end up here." He shrugged.

I gave him a look.

"I'm serious. We have a club and everything. I'm the president. All hail, President Jee."

I shook my head. "I want to believe you're joking, but something tells me your not, which is scary."

"We meet every Tuesday in the basement of a warehouse. It's like Alcoholics Anonymous but cooler, and you know, without the being alcoholic part."

"I'm pretty sure you're psychotic," I muttered under my breath.

"What was that, young Mara?" He cupped a hand around his ear. "I'm fabulous? I know, but thank you for agreeing."

If I'd had solid food I would've thrown it at him, but I didn't want to get soup everywhere so I refrained.

"Do you think she'll speak with us? Victor said we needed to find her." I closed my eyes trying to remember his exact words. It took a moment but they came to me.

"G-Get away f-from here. F-Find C-Cleo. She h-holds the k-key."

"The key to what?" I pleaded, begging him for answers.

"T-The truth."

The truth. What did he mean by that? *What* truth?

He twisted his lips in thought. "She's a bit ... snippy. So it depends on her mood."

"What are the odds we need to find this Cleo person and she's *here?*" Adelaide asked, looking around at all of us. "It's super creepy."

"Like I said, this place is sort of a hub for the weird and strange."

"Why is that?" Winston asked.

Jee thought for a moment. "I guess weird and strange is more easily acceptable in cities. You're always going to find more of it in places like here, New York City, and Los Angeles. We can be ourselves more, and we're also safer because there's a bigger population. The Iniquitous ..." he paused. "People like us are like trophies for them. The Iniquitous are sort of like collectors. The problem is they don't display their pretties on the shelf to look at. They *use* them instead. Force them to do their bidding, or worse turn them to their cause."

"What are they really fighting for anyway? It has to be more than power."

He frowned. "Sadly, power is all that matters to them. Control. Domination. They want to rule over us, turn us into slaves. If they had their choice I'm sure they'd love to rule over *all* magical creatures—fairies, vampires, shifters—but they know their numbers will never be large enough to spread their power that far."

Turning the conversation back to Cleo, I asked, "So do we make an appointment with Cleo or just show up?"

He thought for a moment. "I'd say it's better if we show up. If we tip her off beforehand and she's not interested she may flee, and if she does I can promise you'll never find her. She's a chameleon of sorts."

"Great," I muttered. "We need her, so we can't risk her leaving. The problem is, I don't know what we need her *for*. Victor said to find her—she holds the key to the truth."

"If anyone knows the truth," Jee intoned, "it's Cleo."

chapter thirteen

WE MADE PLANS TO SEE CLEO on Friday.

I counted down the days of the week, eager for answers.

After so much confusion and chaos I felt I deserved to *know* something for a change.

When the day came, I changed my clothes three times before settling on a pair of ripped black jeans, a black shirt, and a leather jacket. I acted as if I was going on a date of some sort, but I wanted this Cleo person to be impressed with me. I wanted her to think I looked badass and worthy of whatever knowledge she needed to bestow upon me.

The five us piled into the Range Rover—Adelaide, Winston, and I squished in the back, while Ethan drove and Jee sat in the passenger seat holding his hand.

Every little bit they'd exchange a doe-eyed love-filled look.

When we arrived at the Mall of America, the place was packed. We drove around for a good thirty minutes before we found a place to park—which we happened upon by luck since someone was backing out.

We followed Jee through the parking garage, to an elevator, and then into the mall.

He seemed to know his way, unlike the rest of us.

"Now, I should warn you Cleo is probably not what you're expecting. So try not to act too surprised."

We walked and walked for what seemed like miles— who knew, maybe it was since this place was *huge*. Adelaide was still oohing and ahhing over the fact there was an amusement park inside the mall when Jee stopped.

"She's around the corner here," he warned. "She'll probably be pissed—she doesn't like to be bothered by us paranormal folk at her place of work, but she can suck it today."

He marched forward again and, like obedient little ducklings, we all followed.

"Hello, Cleo."

Jee stopped at a cart in the center of the mall.

A sign saying *Cleo's Fortune Telling* hung on top of the cart, and there were all kinds of orbs and crystals displayed.

Have your palm read and know your future—does the guy you're crushing on like you back, is your girlfriend cheating, is your fiancé the one, will you die alone? Cleo knows all!

Sitting on a stool with a white and red cane was Cleo.

Like Jee warned, she was not at all what I expected. In my mind, I'd conjured some ancient hunched woman, with a million wrinkles and a gravely voice.

But the real Cleo was young, maybe nineteen with pearly white skin and blonde hair darker than mine with a slight red tint. Her eyes were hid behind a pair of dark sunglasses. That, coupled with the cane, told me she was blind.

"Jee," she hissed under her breath, "why are you here?"

"I brought friends," he explained.

"I can see ... well not *see*, but I know," she griped.

"We—*they*—need to talk to you. It's important."

"Well, I don't want to talk to them." She turned away, giving us her shoulder.

I opened my mouth to argue but Jee gave me a look, silencing me.

"Cleo," he said in a sickly sweet voice, "this is important."

"You've said that once already—twice is repetitive. I'm blind not stupid."

"I never ask you for anything, do I, Cleo?"

She harrumphed, clearly displeased he was indeed right.

"I'm asking for your help now. For my friends. You know I wouldn't be here if it wasn't necessary."

She swiveled back to face us. "I'm not in the habit of giving favors but I suppose this once I can make an exception."

"Thank you." Jee bent and placed a kiss on her cheek.

I swore her cheeks colored pink but it was gone before I could be sure.

"Very well," she muttered. "Let's not do this out in the open."

She placed a closed sign on her cart—like that'd really stop people from stealing—and stood.

"Follow me."

She moved her cane around as she walked, but I got the uneasy feeling she *could* see—just not with her eyes.

She led us through the mall, and down a hallway, through a door and then another before we were in a storage closet. Once the door closed behind us and it was dark she tapped her cane against the cement wall three times in a triangle pattern. The wall melted away and we stepped into a ... home.

The room was painted purple with gauzy curtains, cushions were on the floor with overlapping rugs. There was a mattress in the corner with purple bedding, and a kitchen set up on the opposite wall.

"Welcome to my humble abode." She sunk onto one of the cushions. "Sit, sit," she ushered, oddly pleasant now.

We all did and ended up in a circle with her in the center.

"So, tell me, light one, why are you here?"

"Why do people call me that?" I blurted. It shouldn't have been the question I went with, considering I wasn't sure if she'd accept another.

She lifted her dark glasses on her head and pale, lifeless, blue eyes stared back at me. Her hand lifted in easy dismissal. "Light one, dark one, it's all about the balance really. The balance can't be disrupted without everything going ... Well, let's just say it'd be bad."

"Dark one," I repeated softly. "That's what the Iniquitous called Theo before ... before," I trailed off, not wanting to say before he died.

She smiled, flicking her fingers so hundred of candles littered around the room sprung to life.

"You cannot have the light without the dark. It's all about balance. When the fates align and connect you get two halves of a whole."

This sounded like gibberish to me.

Winston cleared his throat. "Are you saying Mara and Theo are soul bound?"

"Soul bound?" I repeated. "What is that?"

Her lips twitched. "It's when the cosmos create a soul too great, too powerful, for one body to sustain it so they break it apart, and two separate souls are born, but they are in fact one."

"This doesn't mean we're like brother and sister, right?" I nearly gagged at the thought.

No, no, no. It can't be right. I couldn't have fallen in love with my brother of all people.

"No." She laughed like I was silly. "It means you're connected in ways most only dream of."

"Like not even death could separate us?" I whispered, my eyes dropping to the ground.

She frowned. "Yes, not even death could cross such barriers."

I cleared my throat and grabbed the little jar around my neck, holding on tight.

"That's not why we came here."

"I assumed not." She clasped her hands and laid them in her lap.

"When we were fleeing the manor in Seattle, we found Victor. I don't know if you know him—"

"Antonescu?"

"Yes, that's him."

"Continue."

I took a breath. "He was dying, and he told me I had to get away from there and I had to find Cleo. That she— you—held the key to the truth. But I don't know what it is. What's the truth, Cleo?"

Her lips twitched with a slight smile. "I knew you'd come to me one day. Your mother knew too."

"My mother? How do you know my mother? You're my age, right?"

Jee shook his head and laughed.

"Looks can be deceiving, Mara." She pulled her lips back, revealing her teeth, the incisors sharpened to fangs. "I've walked this earth longer than anyone should. It's a lonely life—a half life—but it's my life."

She smoothed her hands over her skirt and looked at me.

"I should warn you, child, the truth is not always easy to accept. Sometimes the truth seems like another lie. Truth is a sword. It cuts you and rips out parts of you you didn't even know you had. But alas, you're here, like the stars foretold, and therefore I'll give it to you."

I held my breath, waiting for her to spill whatever secrets and truth were on the tip of her tongue.

Instead, she stood and walked over to the far wall, fiddling on a bookshelf. She picked up several books, looking inside before shelving them. Finally, she pulled out an emerald green one with a leather bookmark attached and found what she was looking for.

She clasped a small object in her hand and walked over to me.

Opening her hand she held out to me.

"The key."

I stared at the silver key in her hand, weathered with age, and blinked.

When Victor said Cleo had the key to the truth, I thought he meant she *was* the key. I thought I'd get answers. Not more riddles.

She shook her hand. "Take it."

I took it from her and held it in my hand. It was small and surprisingly warm. It almost seemed to hum with energy.

"What's it for?" I asked, looking up at her.

"That, I cannot tell you. You will know when the time comes."

You have to be kidding me.

"Uh ... thanks, I guess."

She laughed. "It'll all make sense in due time."

I touched my fingers to my necklace again, wishing Theo was here, that he'd speak to me, make some joke, do something.

"May I?" Cleo asked.

I nodded.

She clasped my necklace and her eyes rolled back in her head. I almost jerked away from her, but somehow I held still.

She let go and smiled at me, her fangs poking into her bottom lip.

"Oh, it is exactly as the stars have told me. The darkness cowers. I shall celebrate."

"... What?"

I didn't get an answer though, because Cleo then closed her eyes and began to dance around the room.

When she started to take her clothes off, Jee cleared his throat. "We should go. She won't stop this for ..." He looked at an imaginary watch on his arm. "A month or so."

We filed out of the room, and I looked back at Cleo one last time.

The darkness cowers.

I smiled.

Yes, yes it did.

chapter fourteen

SINCE WE WERE ALREADY OUT, Jee and Ethan let us explore the mall for a bit before grabbing a bite to eat and heading back home.

I puzzled over and over the strange key Cleo had given me. I was still baffled by the fact it was an actual *key*.

Lying in bed that night I stared up at the ceiling and turned the key over between my fingers, watching the light glint off of it from the bedside lamp.

Adelaide came into the bedroom and flopped on the bed.

"Can I see it?"

I handed it over.

She studied it too. "What could it be for?"

"I have no idea. I guess it'll all make sense one day."

I felt like I'd ever since I'd stumbled into this world there was always something I couldn't know until I was older, or more wise, or more *something*.

It hardly seemed fair.

If this key was the literal key to something big then why were we waiting?

I mean, we *had* to wait since we didn't know what it unlocked, but it seemed like Cleo could've given us some hint.

Instead, all she said was, *"It'll all make sense in due time."*

What was due time to a vampire? A year? Ten? A century?

Adelaide handed it back to me. "You better put it some place safe. It must be important."

I snorted. "Is any place safe?"

She snapped her fingers and pointed at me "True, boo. *True.*"

We laughed together. I loved these moments. The ones where things were easy and happy, and almost normal. Where I didn't feel the weight of the world on my shoulders, feel the sadness of Theo's loss, or worry about how I was going to survive any of this.

In a war, there are casualties. I'd already seen it firsthand. It wasn't so farfetched to think I could be one too.

I got up from the bed and found my backpack in the closet. Slipping the key into a pocket inside, I zipped it up once more.

Back in bed, I rolled to face Adelaide.

"Do you like Winston?" The words tumbled out of my mouth before I could stop them.

Her whole face turned red. "Is it obvious?"

"No—well, maybe, but he likes you too."

"He does?" she gasped, like this was news to her.

I laughed. "Um, yeah. Are you blind? I'm pretty sure that's why he asked you to the Christmas Eve dance."

"He was being nice."

"Adelaide," I said in a tone implying I thought she was crazy.

"It's weird, though, right? For you? I mean, you dated him."

I snorted. "Can you call it dated? I *tried*, but we both know all I could think about was your brother."

She bit her lip. "I've never done this before. I don't even know how to go about telling him I like him."

I laughed. "Just like that."

She wrinkled her nose. "I can't. It's too weird. Why can't he make the first move?"

"Oh, come on. You're a smart, independent woman. You can tell a guy you like him."

She breathed out heavily. "No, I'm a five-year-old child stuck in an eighteen-year-old's body."

I snorted. "You're insane."

She smiled. "You know you love me."

"I do," I agreed, frowning.

"What's wrong?" She grew serious.

I swallowed thickly. "I was thinking about my friend, Dani, in the human world."

"You miss her?"

I nodded. "Every day. I try not to think of her because it hurts, but I can't help it. I had to leave so suddenly and give her a half-assed story I'm sure she didn't believe," I winced, remembering that stupid phone call. "She probably thinks I hate her, but I don't know how to contact her without risking her being exposed. The Iniquitous must already know who she is, they were at the graduation party I was attending the night Theo found me, and I'm afraid if I keep contact with her ..." I paused and gathered a breath, tears in my eyes. "I'm afraid it'll put an even bigger target on her back. I'll never forgive myself if she's killed because of me."

"Oh, Mara," she breathed, "I'm so sorry."

I brushed a tear away.

"I'm sorry you've lost so much. It's not fair." She frowned, reaching out to grab my hand.

"I can say the same for you."

Sadness overcame her for a moment and then she began to giggle. "Look at us. We're such a sad lot, and why? None of them would want us to be like us. They're probably mocking us for being such cry babies."

I giggled with her. "You're right."

Yeah, she's right.

I gasped. It was the first time I'd heard Theo's voice when I hadn't been practicing magic.

Adelaide stared at me with wide eyes.

"Is it him?" she asked.

I nodded.

He spoke again. *Tell her I love her.*

"He says he loves you."

Tears returned to her eyes. "Can he hear me?"

Theo?

I hear what you hear—so yes.

"He can hear you."

"Oh, my God—Theo, I miss you so much. You have no idea."

"I'm sorry I'm not there."

"He says he's sorry he's not here."

She sniffled. "Is he okay? Wherever he is? What's it like?"

Tell her I'm okay, but I cannot answer the rest.

"He's okay," I promised her.

I have to go, he said suddenly. *I'll meet you in your dreams.*

I wondered what he meant by that, but as I drifted off to sleep I dreamt of a magical garden and the best first kiss anyone could ever ask for.

***

"Again," Ethan commanded.

I roared, slinging my sword into the air; it met with his with a clatter. The sound seemed to vibrate all the way down my arm.

My ponytail swung around my shoulders as I moved.

Like that, Theo spoke in my mind.

My top stuck to my chest, wet with sweat. We'd been at it off and on for hours. Ethan would rotate us out so we'd get short breaks, but it wasn't enough to rejuvenate.

His reasoning was, in a battle we'd have to keep fighting so we might as well start now. This was a taste for what was to come since we were still actually getting a small break.

My arms felt weak, but I kept pushing, refusing to submit.

My stubbornness was a curse and a blessing.

Theo chuckled in my mind. *You are extremely hardheaded.*

Shut up! I screamed at him and he only laughed harder in my mind. *Go away!*

Aw, doll face, you know you love having me here. It's better than not having me at all.

He was right, of course. *You still haven't told me why I can hear you.*

He clucked his tongue. *So many questions. You should know by now how special we are. You can't get rid of me so easy.*

Why were you so quiet in the beginning? It was like it was hard for you to talk.

I managed to have an entire conversation with Theo in my head and focus on fighting Ethan. Talk about multitasking.

I can't tell you.

Why? I ducked, narrowly avoiding a blow to the shoulder from Ethan.

I just can't.

Fine, I huffed.

"Enough," Ethan commanded, and we stopped. "Your turn." He pointed at Adelaide, and she reluctantly stood up.

Adelaide was getting really good with her magic— but combat, not so much.

I personally thought she was too sweet to relish in the feel of a kill, the high of a win. They'd already killed a vital piece of me, maybe the best part, so I had no qualms about ending any of their lives.

I sat by Winston and stretched my legs out. My water bottle sat to the side and I picked it up, gulping it down.

"I think Ethan wants to kill us before we even encounter an Iniquitous."

I snorted. "Yeah, I'm beginning to think the same. But I guess we have to be prepared."

My feet shuffled against the floor before I crossed my ankles. Clearing my throat, I asked, "Did anyone ever know why Thaddeus turned to the Iniquitous?"

His lips twisted in thought. "No," he answered. "He was already a very powerful enchanter, so it was always assumed he wanted more powerful. That's how it happens a lot, you know, people get power hungry. Greed is the strongest motivator."

I pressed my lips together, refusing to speak anything about my supposed brother.

Nobody seemed to know about him so how could he be real? It felt like a ploy by Thaddeus to get me to feel sorry for him. I wouldn't put it past the psycho to make up some story to try and get what he wants.

I was glad I'd only seen him in my dreams twice. Any more, and I was afraid I might go crazy. There was something about him that felt like being drenched in an ice-cold bucket of water.

We each went one more round with Ethan before he finally called it a day.

Exhausted didn't even cover how we felt.

I'd used muscles I didn't even know I had.

When I finally collapsed in bed, I decided to never leave it. It wasn't even late, but I wasn't sure my legs could stand the trek down the steps.

I lay in bed, staring at the ceiling, when Jee cleared his throat roughly from the doorway.

"What?" I spoke, not moving because it'd be painful to even turn my neck.

"I have something for you."

I forced myself to sit up, wincing as I did. "What is it?"

He clasped something behind his back and strode into the room and over to me, sitting on the bed by my feet.

"Here." He held the item out to me and I took it.

It was a small canvas, and painted on it was the profile of a man.

Of *Theo*.

"It came to me," Jee explained, "I didn't know why, or what it meant, but ... I was supposed to give it to you."

I pressed my lips together, fighting tears.

For you, Theo whispered. *I'll find my way back to you.*

I swallowed thickly. *How?*

Nothing and no one can keep me away from you forever. I belong by your side. Not here.

I brushed a tear away. "Thank you," I told Jee, clutching the canvas to my chest. "This means a lot."

Not having any photos of Theo, only memories, this meant more to me than he could begin to fathom. It was only his profile, but it was *him* and that's what mattered most.

"You're welcome." Jee stood from the bed. "I'll leave you be."

I nodded as he left, and I was once more alone. Well, as alone as I could be.

You know, you're more romantic when you're dead.

He busted out laughing. *I'm just as romantic—you didn't get to see this side.*

I frowned glumly. *Don't remind me.*

A soft breeze touched my cheek.

I wish I could touch you.

Lying back on the bed, I closed my eyes.

I miss you, Theo. So much.

I know. I'm sorry it had to be this way. You'll understand one day. My duty will always be to protect you, no matter the cost.

I'd have fought with you.

I know—but you're too important and you know that.

It's not fair. I really only got to love you for one night.

Love beats on, Mara. It doesn't end. It doesn't even really begin. It exists.

His words echoed around my skull and I drew comfort from them.

We had nothing left, nothing but words, but words were powerful and I'd always cherish his.

chapter fifteen

"WE CAN'T KEEP TRAINING FOREVER," I complained, following Ethan around as he tried to avoid me.

He groaned and stepped out of the pantry—his newest hiding spot.

"Mara, we're not ready—*you're* not ready. There are five us and way more of them."

"Four," Jee corrected from the couch, munching on popcorn and watching *Friends*. "This is your battle, not mine. I like my life the way it is."

"Really?" I said with a snarky tone. "Sitting here, day in and day out, rarely leaving this place. You *like* that?"

He turned to glare at me over the back of the couch. "Just because it doesn't sound appealing to you, doesn't mean I don't enjoy it."

I turned my attention back to Ethan who was slowly backing down the hallway.

"Don't think you're getting away so fast," I warned him.

He groaned. "Look, Mara. We don't even know where they are—and you're extremely naïve if you think you can even take on Thaddeus. He's *powerful* and while you're good, you're still a novice."

I crossed my arms over my chest. He was right, but it still bothered me. We were coming up on June, my nineteenth birthday fast approaching, and I still had so much to learn. How was I ever going to get there?

"Fine," I agreed reluctantly. "But can we at least look into finding them?"

Ethan looked away and sighed. Finally, he met my eyes and there was a slight pity there I didn't like. "I have some contacts. I'll make some calls—but if I find out anything I'm not telling you," he warned. "I won't risk you going rogue."

"I wouldn't do that."

He gave me a doubtful look and I grinned.

"Go do something with Adelaide," he told me. "Take the Rover. Get out and be normal for a bit."

I felt the furthest thing from normal, but he was right, it would be nice to get out for a bit.

"If you crash my car," Jee warned, turning again from the couch, "you won't have to worry about Thaddeus killing you. I will."

I rolled my eyes. "Mhmm, sure. I saw you crying over the fly Ethan killed this morning."

He glared at me. "Don't repeat that ever."

I smiled beatifically and headed upstairs to find Adelaide. She was in Winston's room, the two of them talking softly.

"Sorry to interrupt—" They jumped apart and I pretended not to notice. "But I thought we could go out a bit. Do some girl stuff."

"Oh ... um ..." Adelaide faltered, looking from Winston to me. "Yeah, okay. Sounds fun." She hopped up and joined me in the doorway. "I'll see you later." She looked back at Winston with a smile.

He lifted his fingers in a wave. "Later, ladies."

Downstairs, I snagged the car keys from Ethan who held them out with a triumphant smile.

"It'll be nice to get out," Adelaide admitted once we were in the elevator and heading down to the garage. "I feel like I've spent my whole life trapped inside."

"I forget you've never really been out before." I remembered her wide-eyed amazement at the mall.

She cracked a smile. "And it still wasn't safe."

"You've never been to a Starbucks before then, have you?"

"No, definitely not. I've heard of it—the Internet is great for showing you what you can't have."

"That'll be our first stop then."

She grinned. "I can't wait."

I started the car and changed the seat and mirrors before getting acquainted with the set up. It was way fancier than anything I'd driven—even the Lincoln. I searched the navigation system and found the nearest Starbucks, setting it as our destination. It was like a spaceship. When I finally felt comfortable we headed out into the daylight.

With traffic it took us a good twenty minutes to get to Starbucks. Instead of going through the drive-thru I parked and we went inside. I wanted Adelaide to get the whole Starbucks experience.

"Oh, my God, look at all these," she gasped, picking up a mug with the mermaid logo. "They're so pretty. I want them all."

I laughed. "Pick one."

"Are you serious?"

"We can spare the money to get you a mug."

She bit her lip and picked up each and every mug, inspecting every square inch, before finally settling on a mostly blue one with the city skyline boasting the Twin Cities on it.

"This one." She held it out triumphantly like it was some sort of trophy. "It will not only serve as a reminder of my first trip to Starbucks but also our stay here."

We got in line and it took her another ten minutes before she settled on a drink. I ordered my iced latte and paid for both our drinks and the mug—which they boxed, and Adelaide proceeded to ooh and ahh over the box.

We waited off to the side for our order, and Adelaide bounced on the balls of her feet. It was good to see her so happy. She was glum lately and I hadn't really noticed because I'd been too absorbed in my own thoughts. All I could think about was how were we going to stand a chance against Thaddeus. But times like these were important too. I had to remember, I was only eighteen, and before all this I'd been *normal*. It was okay to stop and be ... vulnerable. I didn't have to be on edge, looking for danger, every second of every day.

When we had our drinks we headed back to the car.

"Where to next?" she asked.

I thought carefully. "Have you ever had your nails done?"

"I mean, I've painted them if that's what you're asking."

I shook my head. "No, like at a salon."

"Yeah, that'd be a definite *no*."

"That's where we're headed next then."

It didn't take me long to find a salon—one was right across the street from Starbucks. We opted to do our toes instead of our nails, since with the training it'd be chipped by tomorrow.

150

"This is so weird," Adelaide giggled, as the bubbles engulfed her feet.

The lady doing her feet glared when Adelaide accidently splashed her.

When she went to scrub Adelaide's feet I thought she was going to shoot straight out of her chair, her laughter echoing around the room. "That tickles," she accused.

It took longer than normal, but in the end we left with freshly painted toes. Mine black, and hers a light blue.

From there we headed to the mall. When we'd met Cleo we hadn't been there to shop or look around so I thought Adelaide deserved to get a normal teenage experience.

She excitedly ran from store to store, looking at the items. She was almost childlike, and it was fun to see her so happy.

I hate she didn't get to grow up normal. All she knew was the manor and now she doesn't even have that.

You kept her safe, Theo. That's what matters.

I guess. He didn't sound convinced.

After two hours of going in and out of stores, we went to the food court for a bite to eat.

We set our trays down and Adelaide let out a breath. "I'm already tired and there's still so much to see. We haven't even covered a quarter of this place."

I picked up a fry and popped it into my mouth. "It's way bigger than any mall I've been in, that's for sure."

"So," Adelaide started, a sly smile dancing on her lips. "I've known you almost a year now, but there's a lot I don't really know about you."

I snorted. "I don't know myself, if I'm being honest."

Being thrown into this world the way I had, it felt as if I was an entirely new and different person. The person I was before was gone—she didn't exist.

"Tell me about your *human* life," she whispered the word, her eyes darting around to see if anyone heard. But it was way too loud and chaotic for anyone to hear anything she said.

I shrugged and dipped another fry in ketchup. "I grew up with my dad. We had a quiet life. It was nice. Simple. Easy. He taught me my ABCs, and how to ride a bike." I looked down at the table and tamped down my emotions. It was hard talking about it and knowing those days were gone—my dad was gone.

I'm sorry.

I wish you were here. I wish you could hold me and make me forget, even if only for a little while.

"What's your favorite color?" she asked me, changing the subject since she seemed to sense I was getting upset.

"Purple."

"Did you have a favorite stuffed animal growing up? I had this green monkey I took everywhere. Theodore used to make fun of me for it, but I loved the stupid thing."

I laughed. "I had a rainbow unicorn. I lost it when I was about six or seven—no idea where, but my dad looked and looked for it. He never found it. He tried to get me a new one but it wasn't the same."

"What's a weird quirk you have?"

"I don't think I have one."

She rolled her eyes. "We *all* have one, Mara."

"What's yours then?"

"I brush my teeth without toothpaste then with, and then without again. I like the way it feels."

I snorted. "That's possibly the *weirdest* thing I've ever heard."

She tilted her head. "Come on—we're all weird."

"True," I agreed, thinking of any quirk I might have. "I'm terrified of balloons," I finally admitted. "I once had a dream where my head was stuck inside one and I was suffocating. I've been afraid of them ever since."

"Wow, that's ... um ... interesting."

I tossed a fry at her and laughed. "You brush your teeth *three* times and two of those times isn't even with toothpaste."

"Okay, okay," she chanted. "I admit I can't talk." She took a bite of her food—something from the Chinese restaurant that looked super spicy but she was eating it like it was no big deal. "What about *human* schools?" she whispered again. "What are they like?"

"Pretty boring," I admitted. "It's just stuff like history and math." I shrugged and took a bite of my burger. "Once you get into middle and high school you get to pick electives—stuff like art and woodshop," I added when she raised a brow inquisitively.

"I had a tutor at the manor, since I was young, and it was like that too—boring stuff, like our histories, language arts, Latin."

"What was it like growing up there?"

"Quiet." She frowned. "I really only had Theodore. The adults didn't have time for orphans like us—so we only had each other."

"That's so sad."

She forced a smile. "It wasn't so bad. He was a great brother—yeah, we fought like any siblings, but we got along better than most too."

"I'm sure you guys got into a lot of trouble there."

She snorted. "Oh, Theodore *definitely* did. He was a troublemaker right from the start. I'm sure Victor would've loved to have kicked him out right from the start, but since it's a safe house he can't refuse a right to stay unless there's just cause and all the stuff Theodore did was dumb, prank kind of things."

"Tell me one," I begged, desperate to know about a younger Theo.

"Well, this one time—"

Oh, no, Theo sighed.

"His friend snuck these firecracker things in when he got back from visiting his aunt or something, so

Theodore got the bright idea to strap one to the manor cat—"

"It didn't kill the cat, did it?" I gasped.

"No, no," she assured me with a wave of her hand. "Anyway, so the cat goes running straight down the hall to where Victor's office is. Runs smack into him and climbs up him as the firework goes off." She laughed heartily at the memory. "I have never seen Victor so mad before. A whole patch of hair was burnt off."

"That sounds like Theo." I wished her story made me feel happier than it did, but all I could think about was how fun and *alive* he'd been, and now he was no more than a voice trapped inside my head.

I'm not trapped, doll face. I'm here because I want to be.

"Do you like driving?" she asked me. "I was never allowed to learn."

"Yeah, I do. I miss my dad's old truck."

That piece of shit? Really? Why?

Just because you didn't appreciate it doesn't mean I didn't.

But it was a piece of crap.

It was my dad's piece of crap, I argued and he grew quiet.

"Do you think you could teach me sometime?"

"Yeah, of course," I told her. "I'm not sure Jee will offer up his car for you to learn in, but we'll figure it out."

"Cool." She smiled and her normally dark blue eyes were brighter than normal—happy. It was good to see her like this. "Let me think of another question." She pierced a piece of her chicken with her fork and took a bite. She chewed and swallowed before finally asking, "What's the best present you've ever been given?"

I removed the jar necklace from beneath my shirt and held it out.

"Theo gave this to me for my birthday last year. It's the greatest gift I've ever been given."

She reached out and touched the jar. "H-He gave this to you?" she asked.

"Yeah?" I questioned.

"Where'd he get it?"

"He made it—that's why it means so much. It makes me feel like I'm still close to him. Like in some small way I can hold him."

She began to cry.

"Adelaide," I startled at her tears, "why are you crying?"

"If he made that, if that's *his* firefly, then ..."

"Then what?" I prodded.

"He's alive."

chapter sixteen

ER WORDS WASHED OVER ME like a
bucket of ice water.

I sat, frozen, processing her words over
and over again.

He's alive.

He's alive.

He's alive.

You're alive? I accused. *You're alive and you didn't tell me?* I was beyond hurt.

Mara, I was trying to protect you.

Protect me? I shrieked at him. *Protect me from what? You've been speaking to me all this time and I thought you were* dead. *I thought you were a ghost or something, and you let me believe it!*

Mara, please, he begged. *You know your safety means more to me than my own life. I couldn't let you risk your life to save mine.*

Fat lot of good it does now. Where are you? I need to find you.

NO! he shouted so forcefully I literally felt the words reverberate around my skull.

Theo, my mind sobbed. *Don't say that. If you're alive we can come for you. We can—*

I told you I'd find my way back to you and I will. I'm working on it. But you need to stay away.

Don't do this. You're being stupid. We can find you—we can save you.

Mara, I could've left any time I wanted, he growled angrily. *Some things are worth the risk.*

What do you mean?

Knowledge, Mara. It's the most powerful weapon we hold. I'm coming back to you. I always was. But not yet.

I felt him slip from my mind.

Theo! THEODORE! I yelled, but he wasn't there anymore, and I didn't know how to slip into *his* mind.

Adelaide was sobbing across from me and gathering more than one stare.

"We should go," I said, and dumped our food in a nearby trashcan before dragging her from the food court and to the garage we'd parked in.

I was sweating from nerves, from the fact Theo was *alive*.

In the moment, I hated him.

I hated him for speaking inside my mind for *months* and not once giving me a hint he was alive. He knew how much I ached for him, how I *mourned*, and he let me.

I wanted to say I couldn't forgive him but I'd be lying.

Adelaide cried the whole way back, I couldn't even talk to her to tell her what he'd said to me.

Where was he? Why could he leave at any time? Surely, if the Iniquitous had taken him he couldn't just walk out? What did all this mean?

I parked the Range Rover and dumped our Starbucks out into a trashcan since I knew the wrath of Jee wasn't worth leaving them there, and grabbed our stuff—the Starbucks bag and a few odd things we picked up at the mall.

The ride up in the elevator was the longest of my life.

"What's wrong?" Ethan asked running down the hall to us at the sound of Adelaide crying.

"She's fine," I assured him. "She's not hurt."

Winston collided into the back of Ethan and quickly righted himself, pulling Adelaide into his arms. She clung to him like her life depended on it.

"What's all this sniffling about?" Jee asked, walking down the hall with Nigel in his arms. The cat had taken an uncanny liking to Jee I couldn't begin to fathom.

"What's wrong with her?" Winston asked over the top of Adelaide's head.

I sighed and dropped the bomb. "Theo's alive."

They all gaped at me like I expected.

"What the fuck?" Ethan blurted. "Are you serious?"

I nodded. "Deadly." *No pun intended.*

"How'd you find out?" Winston asked. "Did he tell you in ... uh ..." He pointed to his head and I shook mine.

"No, Adelaide figured it out."

She pulled away from Winston to point at my necklace. "Her necklace, Theo made it, it's his firefly. If he'd died, it would have too."

"Jeez." He held her a little closer. "Who knew this whole time we could've known he was alive?"

I clutched my necklace and felt silly I hadn't known, but there was no way I could have. All I'd known was it was an enchanted firefly. I figured they lived forever— or at least an extra long life.

"Why wouldn't Theodore tell you he was alive?" Winston asked me over the top of Adelaide's head.

"He said he was protecting me, because he knew I'd try to find him. He also said he could get away at any time, but some things were worth the risk. Whatever that means."

Winston exchanged a look with Ethan. "They must've taken him wherever Thaddeus is," he supplied. "That's the only thing I can think of that would keep him from leaving."

"How can he leave, though?" My voice was almost shrill. "Surely they have him guarded, locked away somewhere."

Ethan shook his head. "If Theodore said he could get out, it means he can."

"How?"

Jee stepped forward. "He's a protector, he's *your* protector, his powers far outweigh those we know to be true."

"This is all so confusing," I muttered. "I clearly didn't learn enough about where we came from, about protectors, about *any* of this."

"Come." Jee motioned. "Story time."

***

He led us all to the training room where we sat in a circle. He waved his hand a fire appeared in the circle floating above the circle.

He smiled. "I always loved a good campfire and story."

He cleared his throat. "Enchanter's powers can be traced back to an ancient line of Wiccan power, thousands of years ago. They were first recorded in Egypt—believed to be Gods and Goddesses, bringing destruction and despair, happiness and health. As time went on, they moved around the world, spreading, growing in numbers. I'm sure you've all heard of the Salem Witch Trials?" he asked and waited for us to nod. "Those were the times when the Iniquitous first began to rise. Our friends, family, no one could be trusted. Those who turned to the dark side poked fingers at their fellow enchanters who wouldn't convert, and they were persecuted. Many of those who were executed were mere mortal, but the hysteria had grown substantially within the human race and they saw evil everywhere.

"Over the years, the enchanters and Iniquitous separated and lived ... almost peacefully, neither bothering the other. But around two hundred years ago, the Iniquitous began hunting them down and those they could not convince to join their side were slaughtered. It was a messy time, a frightful time, one where many enchanters feared leaving their house and didn't know who to trust.

"That's when the war first began. Our numbers were large then, and they fought back. United, their powers were more than the Iniquitous could handle. Many died on both sides, but in the end the Iniquitous retreated into the shadows like the monsters they are.

"Things became peaceful again and stayed that way for a long time. Some began to think the Iniquitous had died out, but others knew they'd be back one day. A strong enchanter came along, his powers unparalleled. Handsome and charismatic he could charm the pants off anyone. Many talked about making him King—"

"Is there royalty?" I asked.

"Up until then, no, but many loved him and felt to give him the title would signal the end of the Iniquitous. That we were united and powerful, with the best of the best. But then greed took over. When you possess so much power, you can't help but covet more. That desire takes over until it consumes you." He stared at me and I shivered. It was like he was taking about me—*warning* me. "Thaddeus craved more power and he sought out any means to get it, even if it changed him in the process. Turned and twisted his insides until they were barely recognizable.

"There's no coming back from it, once you've gone down that path. He turned on his fellow enchanter, killing many of them. He didn't even try to convert them to his side, he didn't care, he wanted them *dead*."

"You're talking about Thaddeus, aren't you?" I interrupted.

"Yes—I fled just in time. He was my friend, you know. I admired him, we grew up together, but I saw something change in his eyes one day and I knew I had to get away. If I'd stayed, I'm certain he'd have killed me first. He must assume I'm dead, or he would've tried to find me. I've been good about keeping my identity hushed. Your mother left too, she knew it wasn't safe to be near him, and I guess especially not if she was pregnant with you. She was a kind woman, pure, she would've turned to the dark side. Not for him, not for anything."

"But she loved him—I mean, she had to, right?"

Jee bit the inside of his cheek. "Yes, I suppose she did, but I always wondered ... Never mind." He shook his head.

"What?" I probed.

"I always wondered if there was another who stole her heart."

Back to his story, he continued, "Once Celeste fled, Thaddeus spiraled even more out of control. Enchanters fought against him, but he possessed powers we'd never seen before. Many died, and thus the second war began, and it's never really ended. It's fought much more quietly these days, so as not to attract human attention, or attention to themselves. But there's an underground faction of enchanters who follow the movements of the Iniquitous, know the ins and outs of their hideouts, and take them out one by one when they can. It's not an all-out slaughter like you may assume, or even want, but it is *smart*. By not drawing attention to themselves they're able to kill much more effectively."

"I was with them," Ethan piped up. "Before I went back to the manor. They sent me there to keep an eye out, they got word the Iniquitous were planning to invade the safe houses. They wanted me to be a lookout. Theodore knew where I'd gone, and he assumed why I returned—I ended up telling him, of course—that's why he trusted me with you."

"Do they have a name?" I asked.

"They call themselves The Hood," Ethan replied.

"How'd you find them?"

"They found me actually." I raised a brow and he began to explain. "They hear about promising enchanters, and then ... well, I guess they sort of spy on you, to see if you're indeed on the right side. Then they send you a letter, welcoming you, with a place to meet them if you accept their invitation."

"Sounds like a fraternity to me."

"A what?" he asked, puzzled.

"Never mind."

"Anyway," he continued, "The Hood hunts down Iniquitous and kills them quietly. They have people on the inside too."

"How do they, you know, not go bad?" Adelaide asked.

Ethan shrugged. "I'm sure it happens, or could if it hasn't. But they get a lot of their Intel that way."

"What are we going to do about Theo?" I asked. "We know he's alive, we have to get him." I looked around the circle at my friends. Adelaide was the only one who nodded excitedly with me.

"Mara," Ethan began slowly, "if he said he could get away at any time then we have to trust he'll come when he's accomplished whatever it is he's trying to do."

"You have to be kidding me," I cried, exasperated. "He's alive and you expect me to *wait*."

"Mara—"

"*No.*" I stood up and glared at the three guys. "I can't believe you expect me to be okay leaving him *there*. Wherever *there* is. You know they must be hurting him."

I turned on my heel and fled from the room, up the stairs, and to my bedroom.

I felt like crying, hurt radiating in my chest as I fought tears. How'd they think I could be okay with finding out he was alive and doing *nothing?*

Hugging my pillow to my chest, I lay on my stomach.

A soft brushing against my mind told me Theo had entered it.

Go away. I snarled at him.

He didn't say anything, but he didn't leave, either, and secretly I felt better having him there.

chapter seventeen

ARE YOU STILL IGNORING ME?

It's been a week.

Mara, stop being childish.

"I need a break," I told Winston, and the leaves I'd been levitating off the ground fell back down to the earth.

I walked off, where I'd be to myself, but still within the safety of the bubble Ethan had us enclosed in.

Scuffing along, I found a stump and took a seat on it.

I'm mad at you.

Ah! She speaks!

Don't be a smart ass. I'm hurt, you know it. How could you let me believe for six months you were dead?

It's what I had to do.

What if you thought I was dead for six months and I'd had the opportunity to tell you but hadn't? How would it make you feel?

He growled in my mind. *I'd be livid.*

Exactly.

He huffed. *You do realize we argue like an old married couple, right?*

I rolled my eyes. *And you do realize we're not married, we're barely even a couple, right?*

Barely even a couple? Pretty sure we've established we are.

A good boyfriend wouldn't let his girlfriend think he's dead.

I was—

Protecting me, I sneered in a mocking tone. *I know. That's always your excuse. When will you learn to trust me? I might be young and new to this world, but I've already gone through a lot. You don't have to keep secrets from me.*

Yes, I do, if I know by telling you you'll do something reckless or stupid—most likely both.

That's not fair. You don't even give me a chance.

You forget I know you—almost better than I know myself. I can read you like an open book, and I know there's no way, if I'd told you I was alive and to wait until I was ready to come back, that you'd have listened. You would've done everything to rescue me and ended up hurting, or worse killing, yourself in the process. Can't you be happy I'm alive? Or would you rather I was dead?

Don't. You. Dare. Say. That. I spat out. *You know there's no way I'd want you to be gone. You have no idea what I felt watching ... watching the sword go through your body. I felt like I was dying with you. I've never felt pain like it, and I wasn't even the one hurt.*

I'm sorry. His words were soft, almost apologetic, but not quite. This *was* Theo after all. *It was never my intention to hurt you or cause you any pain—and I understand what you mean, if the situation was reversed I wouldn't be happy with you either. But the information I can get is worth my staying.*

At least answer me this, are they hurting you?

He grew quiet. *I can't answer you.*

They are then. I shook my head, toeing the dirt. A stubborn dandelion was budding its way through.

I can take it.

You shouldn't have to.

I don't *have to. I can leave, I promise you.*

How can you leave? I don't think they're going to let you walk away.

I'm a special protector.

I've heard you say that before—but why? How?

I can't explain it now, but I have powers most dream of, some would say powers that aren't supposed to exist. I promise you, I can get out of here undetected and come to you.

Do you know where I am?

Yes, I can see through your eyes if I want, but even if I couldn't I'd find you. I can always feel you, Mara. Sense you. You can't get away from me so don't even think about it.

I laughed. *I wouldn't even try—though, I might enjoy you chasing me.*

Admit it, doll face, you want me on top of you.

I smiled at the familiarity of him joking. *I miss you.*

He sighed inside my mind. *I miss you too.*

Whatever you're doing, hurry back to me, please.

I will.

I felt him slip from my mind, and I instantly missed his presence. Not talking to him the last week had been hard, especially knowing he was actually alive. But I was hurt, and I was having trouble with the fact he let me think he was dead. I'd needed some time to myself to think, but I'd still felt him there at times.

I stood up and brushed the back of my shorts off and headed back to Winston.

"Ready?" he asked me, dropping the stick he'd been playing with.

"Yeah," I sighed.

I didn't feel ready at all. My heart wasn't as invested anymore, not now that I knew Theo was alive.

But they couldn't be allowed to exist in our world and get away with what they'd done—the slaughter of the New York and Seattle safe houses. We hadn't been able to get an official word on what happened in Seattle, but having been there we could assume.

I still wanted to see them suffer, to cower and pay, but the urgency was gone.

Now, I felt like we had more time.

More time to learn.

More time to train.

More time to strategize.

My thoughts circled back to The Hood, and I wondered if Ethan could get word to them we wanted to help. I wasn't sure they'd want to take us on, since we were kind of a hot mess. But hey, we were getting there.

Winston and I started practicing again. Instead of levitating the leaves he had me move on to sticks.

"That's good," he coached. "Now throw it."

"Are you going to catch it, Air Bud?"

"Funny."

"I'm impressed you knew what I was referring to."

"I grew up in the human world," he reminded me. "I'm not like her." He tossed a thumb in the general direction of Adelaide.

I threw the stick with my mind, and it soared through the air, landing out of sight.

"Good." He clapped his hands. "I want to get to the point where you can levitate and throw people."

"Now, I'm intrigued." I smirked and spread my feet wider.

He pulled an item out of the bag he'd brought with us and set it down. It was a box of Nigel's cat treats.

"You know Nigel is going to be pissed if we lose his treats." I raised a brow at Winston.

He scoffed. "We can buy him more."

I stared at the box and it lifted easily into the air. I held it there for a few seconds, my hands held out in front of me, and then when I moved my hands the box went with them flying through the air at rapid speed. Dropping my hands, the box dropped too and fell to the ground several yards from us.

And so it went.

Next he pulled out a hammer, then an encyclopedia, and last a blender.

A freaking *blender* of all things.

When I successfully levitated and threw all of them he beamed with pride.

"Now you're going to try with me."

"With you?" I squeaked. "I don't want to hurt you."

He waved a dismissive hand. "What's a few scrapes and bruises?"

"Winston," I whined with nerves. I didn't want to hurt him, and he was way heavier than anything I'd levitated so far, so chances were this was going to end bad.

I felt Theo prick my mind. *Hang him by his foot and shake him.*

Go away, you're not helping.

Laughing, he retreated from my mind.

"You can do this, Mara," Winston urged. "Don't overthink it."

I frowned but closed my eyes. Somehow, by closing my eyes, I always seemed to find my way better.

Inhaling a deep breath, I let it out slowly.

Winston grew quiet, letting me work through it on my own. He was good like that; instead of pushing me to do something he let me think it through.

After a moment, I opened my eyes and held my hands out.

I pictured lifting him into the air like he was light as a feather.

Nothing happened.

I tried again.

I could feel my mental walls shaking with the effort.

"You're too heavy," I complained, teeth gritted as I tried to lift him.

"Mara," he said softly, "you're stronger and more powerful than you think you are. You can do this. You can do anything."

He was right—my doubting myself wasn't helping anything.

I was strong, I was powerful, I was capable.

I was a warrior.

I had to be confident in myself if I was ever going to be ready to take on the Iniquitous and Thaddeus.

Centering myself, I felt my magic flow through my belly and up through my arms, coursing out of me.

Winston lifted off the ground and hooted with pleasure.

With a groan, I slung his body and he hit a nearby tree, falling to the ground.

"Oh, my God, Winston!" I cried, running over to him and dropping to my knees beside him. "Are you okay? I'm so sorry."

He laughed and shook some debris out of his hair. "Don't be sorry, that was incredible. A couple of bruises are worth it. I want to try something else."

He stood up and tried to hide a grimace of pain from me.

"Hey, Ethan?" he called over, and Ethan ceased what he was doing with Adelaide. "Can you help me with something?"

Ethan nodded and said something to Adelaide before jogging over to us. "I want Mara to practice levitating and throwing the both of us."

"What?" I backed away. "No, no, no." I swung my hands in a slashing motion. "I could barely lift you, there's no way I can do both of you."

"Mara," he said warningly and I took a breath. "If we encounter a huge group of Iniquitous this comes in handy. The more you can shove out of the way the better."

I let out a heavy breath. "Okay, we'll try it, but if you both end up high in a tree I'm *not* getting you down."

He chuckled. "I have faith in you."

I backed away from them and they stood in front of me, about four feet between them.

Inhaling, I took a moment to gather my thoughts.

You can do this. No more doubting yourself.

With a groan, I felt my magic welling up inside me once more. Roaring, I shoved my hands out and the magic blasted out of me.

I didn't even levitate them, but the force shoved them fifty feet away from me and out of the bubble we were protected in.

My hands dropped and so did my jaw.

They returned clapping. Both of their hair was sticking up in every direction and their clothes were ruffled and covered in leaves and bits of grass.

"Bravo," Winston chortled. "I can't wait to see you in battle."

"You think I'm ready?" I asked.

He shrugged. "I could teach you new things for the next two years if I wanted, but you're a natural and I think most things will come to you easily in the moment. You're powerful for your age, that's for sure."

I smiled, pleased by his praise.

Some days, I felt successful, and others I felt like I was never going to get there.

We packed up and headed home for the day.

My thoughts drifted back to my dream about Thaddeus and his words about me having a brother. I wanted to believe he was lying, no one seemed to know about this child or they would've said something, but why would he? He didn't stand to gain anything by telling me that.

If Theo was where Thaddeus was, maybe this was what was keeping him there. Or maybe he'd discovered my mom alive and was trying to figure out how to leave with her too. I wasn't sure what I'd do or how I'd feel if she was alive. I mean, she was my mom after all, but I didn't really know her.

There were so many unknowns right now, but one thing I was certain of was I'd have to confront Thaddeus eventually, and Theo wasn't going to be one bit happy about it.

chapter eighteen

"HAPPY BIRTHDAY TO ME," I sang softly, looking out the window of my bedroom. It didn't feel like my birthday at all. If I hadn't seen the day reflecting at me on the calendar in the room I would've forgotten.

Things had changed drastically in the last year. I felt like an entirely new person. I was stronger, but hardened to the world. What I'd seen was a drop in the bucket to what the Iniquitous were capable of, but it was enough to change me.

After a while, I forced myself to get dressed and head downstairs.

"You guys," I paused, overcome by emotion.

Jee, Ethan, Adelaide, and Winston all stood in the kitchen, surrounded by homemade pancakes and a strawberry cake.

I shook my head. "You didn't have to do this."

"Did you think we'd forget?"

"It's just another day," I sighed. "I wouldn't blame you if you did."

Adelaide looked at me like I was crazy. "You're our friend. We love you. It's *not* another day to us."

"But—" Winston held up a finger in warning "—don't think this means you get out of practice today. We're working on a freezing spell."

I smiled. "Wouldn't dream of it."

Pulling out one of the stools, I took a seat and Adelaide handed me a plate piled high with pancakes.

"For the record, I didn't make those so if they're shit you can't blame me. I'm only here because I look fabulous in an apron and chef's hat." Jee patted the hat on his head fondly. My lips twitched from withheld laughter.

I poured some syrup onto the pancakes and took a bite. "They're delicious. Thank you."

The others each grabbed a plate, and Adelaide sat on the stool beside me while the others leaned against the counter.

Theo's absence bothered me, but I tried not to let it show. He'd been silent the last few days and I was worried.

What if something happened?

What if Thaddeus killed him for real this time?

Why *was he kept alive to start with?*

I forced those thoughts out of my mind, refusing to let my worries bring me down, not when my friends had gone out of their way to make today special for me.

"How does it feel to be nineteen?" Winston asked me.

I laughed and thought for a moment, trying to come up with a serious answer. "It feels ... overwhelming," I admitted.

"Why?" He raised a brow.

"I have this feeling like something going to happen. It's been too quiet, if that makes any sense."

"I hope you're wrong," he replied, but I saw in his eyes he was worried too.

My eyes sought Jee and I found him looking down at his plate, his shoulders tense.

Slowly, he raised his head and when he looked at me I felt ice in my veins.

He'd seen something.

***

"I'm stuffed," I declared, setting my cake plate down. "How you expect me to practice magic after this is beyond me. I need a nap."

The cake had been delicious—so much so, I'd had two slices.

"You're not getting out of it that easy," Ethan warned.

"But it's my birthday," I whined.

Winston chuckled. "And you're the reason we're all doing this, so nice try."

I smiled. He was right, after all. "Fine, okay. Let's go."

"Do we have to?" This time it was Adelaide complaining. "I'm with Mara. I need a nap."

Ethan shook his head. "Nice try, girls. We're going." He pointed in the direction of the elevator.

"Be safe," Jee whispered to him, and the two exchanged a quick kiss.

The four of us piled into the Range Rover, the guys in the front, with us in the back.

"I still haven't mastered levitating like you did." Adelaide frowned, her brows drawn. "I feel like I'm never going to get it."

"It's hard," I agreed. "I had to stop overthinking it."

"I thought finally coming into my magic was going to be *fun*, but with all that's going on it's really kind of scary, knowing I'm going to have to use it against the Iniquitous. I feel naïve for thinking I'd never have to face them."

I reached for her hand and she smiled at me. "We're in this together. You don't have to be afraid of them."

"I know," she replied, and gave my hand a slight squeeze.

Adelaide was the sister I never had and I worried about her. She was kind, and warm hearted, with a whole lot of sass thrown in, but I didn't want any of this to change her. Not the way it had me. I knew at my core I was still *me*, but I'd changed so much. Even though I knew Theo was alive now, it was impossible to shake how watching a sword go into him had changed me.

Vengeance still burned brightly in my veins.

For Steven Pryce, the man who'd always be my real dad to me, for all the innocent enchanters they'd slaughtered, and for justice.

Too long had they terrorized enchanters, and it needed to end.

I was new to this world, but I didn't think it was right for them, for *us*, to be afraid.

Maybe this was what I was born for, why I was chosen.

Could it be possible I was born for the sole purpose of killing my biological father and destroying the Iniquitous once and for all?

Ethan parked the car and we all hopped out, making the trek through the woods.

The sun shone through the trees, the green leaves glimmering. The air was warm, in the seventies, with a slight breeze.

I smiled as I watched a bunny hopping after a squirrel. The squirrel darted around and then ran up a tree and stood on a branch. The brown bunny stared up at squirrel in the tree before hopping away.

We stepped into the bubble and separated.

Winston laid his duffel bag on the ground and straightened to look at me.

"Freezing spells are pretty easy, but we're going to start with small objects first. I'll demonstrate."

He bent down and unzipped the bag, pulling out an apple. He tossed it to me and I caught it.

"I want you to throw this toward me like you would a baseball and I'm going to freeze it. Watch me, okay?" He waited for me to nod. "Okay, now."

I threw the apple and he thrust his right hand out, his fingers spread.

It halted in mid air.

He waved his hand and it unfroze, soaring into his hands.

"Ready to try?" he asked.

"Yeah, I'm ready." I shook out my hands to get rid of my jitters.

He tossed it and on instinct I pushed both hands out in front of me.

The apple exploded into a million tiny pieces, the juice spraying over the both of us.

"Well," he laughed, "it seems you're good at explosion spells but that's not what I was going for." He wiped a piece of apple off his cheek and dropped it on the ground.

"Sorry," I said sheepishly, brushing some apple gunk off my arms.

He pulled another apple out of the bag. "Ready?"

I adjusted my stance and flexed my fingers. "Yeah."

He tossed the apple and I saw in my mind how he'd done it and mimicked his gesture. This time the apple stopped and hung suspended in the air.

"I did it!" I cried, but as soon as I lowered my hand it dropped to the ground. "Oh." I frowned.

"It's okay," he assured me. "You need to feel it more."

"Feel it more," I repeated. "Right. I can do that."

I took a breath to calm and center myself.

Winston picked up the apple and returned to where he'd been standing.

I nodded when I was ready and he threw the apple into the air.

I did the exact same thing I did before, but this time I *felt* it. I threw my entire body into stopping the apple and when I lowered my hand it stayed where it was floating in the air.

"Excellent." Winston grinned and clapped.

I waved my hand like he had before and the apple started moving again. I caught it and tossed it back to him.

We did it a few more times before moving on to another larger item—a basketball, which I had no idea where he'd gotten.

Something began to prickle along my skin—some sort of awareness.

I looked down at my arm and the fine blonde hairs were sticking straight up.

"What's wrong?" Winston asked, picking up on my behavior.

"Someone's here," I whispered.

He paled and motioned for Ethan, telling him what I said, while I looked around wildly.

"We should be safe inside the bubble," Ethan began. "No one should be able to see us or get inside."

I looked around wildly, my whole body humming with awareness.

None of it seemed to make any sense, I couldn't see anyone but I knew they were there.

My heart beat went out of control.

I glanced at the others. "It's Theo," I declared. "He's here."

Before they could blink, I took off running. "No, Mara!" Ethan called after me. "It could be a trap!"

"Mara! Adelaide, stop!" Winston screamed too, but their words fell on deaf ears.

Theo was here. I knew it and felt it with every fiber of my being. That wasn't something I could ignore. I ran as hard and as fast as I could. Thanks to all the physical training I'd been doing I wasn't even winded.

I ran and ran, stumbling over roots and twigs, but nothing was going to stop me.

I knew I'd left the shelter of the bubble, but the others still called from behind me.

They sounded far away, though, and I didn't know how I'd run *that* fast. It was like my feet were forcing their way through the earth, being dragged like a magnet, back to the one they belonged to—to the person I was meant to stand beside, always.

And then, between two trees I spotted him.

He wore a black cloak, the hood drawn up. His head was slightly lowered, but I couldn't help but notice his hair now hung past his ears.

"Theo." I crashed into him, the two of us colliding with a force that could rival tectonic plates.

His arms wrapped around me and he buried his face into the crook of my neck. He inhaled deeply, and his breath fluttered against my neck.

"You're here," I breathed. "You're really here."

"I told you I'd come back to you." He took my face between his hands and looked me over. I noticed the dark circles under his eyes, and how gaunt he looked, like he was malnourished. "You look good."

"And you look like a caveman," I joked, lightly tugging on his beard.

He traced a finger over my lips. "You're more beautiful than I remember."

"It's a new shampoo," I teased with a smile. "It gives my hair extra bounce."

My smile quickly disappeared, though. There was no telling what he'd been through the last six months. Horrors, I probably couldn't even begin to comprehend, and here I was joking like nothing at all had happened.

He cracked a half smile.

"Theodore!"

Adelaide collided with us and the three of us fell to the forest floor. We'd been so absorbed in each other we hadn't even heard her, which wasn't good. *Anyone* could've snuck up on us.

"Ade," he chuckled as the three of us tried to untangle ourselves. "I thought you would've been happy I was gone."

She smashed her closed fist against his chest and I wiggled away.

"How dare you say such a thing, you jerk. You're my brother, of course I missed you, you big idiot."

"And there's the little sis I know and love."

"Ugh, you're such an asshole. Why am I even glad you're back?"

She stood up and brushed dirt from her clothes.

Theo stood and offered me a hand. Once upon a time I would've refused his help, but now I wanted an excuse to touch him, because he was *here*. He was *alive*.

That meant more than anything else.

"Hey, man. It's good to have you back." Ethan clapped hands with him.

"Yeah, good to see you mate." Winston jerked his chin in a nod, but I got the impression he wasn't happy at all he was back, especially when his eyes drifted to Adelaide and quickly away.

I found myself clinging to Theo, afraid if I let go he'd vanish. His hood had fallen in the scuffle and leaves clung to his hair. I picked it out and he smiled at me.

"Happy birthday," he whispered.

I'd completely forgotten. "I can't believe you're here." I kept saying basically the same thing over and over again, but I couldn't get over it.

For six months he'd been *gone*, and for the majority of it I believed him dead, even when I started hearing his voice.

"I'd never miss your birthday." He skimmed his fingers over my cheek. "Never," he repeated, and I got the impression he was speaking more for himself than me. His eyes flickered over my face, taking in the small differences that had appeared since the last time I saw him. Tearing his eyes from me, Theo addressed Ethan, "We have a lot to talk about. Can we head back to Jee's?"

"You know about Jee?" Ethan blurted, perplexed.

"I could see through Mara's eyes when I wanted, and hear too, so yes, I know."

Ethan shook his head and muttered something about *super freaky weird protector powers* under his breath.

Theo smirked at me and I felt myself exhale a sigh of relief.

Despite the change in his appearance, and how it worried me, he was still himself and it's what mattered most.

The five of us made the several-mile trek back to the car in record time, or maybe it felt that way since I was holding Theo's hand for a change.

I'd never been able to hold his hand like this, not even on our last night.

We'd fought so hard to stay apart, and I still didn't understand the reasons why—I didn't think Theo understood it, either—that something as small as holding hands was monumental. It made me cherish the small things with him, the simple things. Every touch, every glance, was more meaningful. It packed a bigger punch.

The five of us piled into the car, Theo, Adelaide, and I squished into the backseat, while Ethan drove us back to the apartment.

Theo being back was going to change things, I hoped it wasn't in a bad way.

With Theo, you never knew, but right then, having him back was more important than what might happen.

chapter nineteen

THEO WANTED TO TAKE A shower first thing when we arrived at the apartment.

Jee didn't even bat an eye when Theo walked in, and I figured he must've seen him coming—but he sure didn't tell us anything, jerk.

I sat on the couch, my legs bouncing restlessly while we waited for Theo to return.

He promised to tell us what he'd learned while he was with Thaddeus. As much as I was anxious to hear it, I also didn't want to know. I was sure there were parts which weren't pleasant, and learning about how he'd been hurt and treated made me queasy.

"Calm down," Adelaide scolded, placing her hand on my knee to stop the bouncing.

"I'm sorry." I gave her a sheepish smile.

"Lay down," she coaxed. "You need some rest."

I nodded and did as she said, cupping my hands under my head.

I doubted I'd fall asleep but somehow I did.

"Where is he?" Thaddeus thundered, spinning around a dark room. It smelled of mold and looked like a prison with cinderblock walls, concrete floors, and bars on the tiny window which looked out onto the world.

"We don't know, sir. He shouldn't have been able to get out."

Two men stood in front of Thaddeus. One with dark hair was staring straight at him, unafraid. The other, shorter and with blond hair, stared at his feet.

"You imbeciles, you must've done something." Thaddeus's nostrils flared with anger.

The dark haired one shook his head. "No, sir. This door has not been open since yesterday. He must've had help."

"We needed him—he was our leverage to get the girl. She's the key to this. Without her, I cannot succeed."

Thaddeus shook his head back and forth, his fists tight at his sides. Suddenly, he roared at the ceiling, the sound echoing off the walls.

A blast of power came out of him, uncontrolled it seemed, and I watched in horror as the two men were reduced to dust.

"Ulysses," he called in a sharp, commanding tone.

It wasn't long until a tall slender man appeared at his side. His hair was a shade of gray almost appearing lavender but his face was free of wrinkles.

"Yes?" he drawled.

Unlike the others this man didn't appear afraid of Thaddeus. Instead, he seemed oddly amused.

"We need a new plan," he growled. "This one has failed. We cannot fail again, do you hear me?"

Ulysses smirked. "What do you propose we do?"

"You figure it out. The protector is gone and he was my greatest hope of getting her."

Thaddeus stormed from the room, his shoulder bumping the other man's roughly.

Ulysses began to laugh, and I began to scream.

"Mara, Mara! Wake up! It's just a dream!"

My eyes burst open to a frightened Adelaide standing over me, her blue eyes wide with fear. Winston was pale beside her.

Across the room, Jee spoke in an unaffected tone, "Stop crowding her. She'll be fine in a moment. Here." He stepped up beside me and handed me a piece of chocolate. "Eat it."

I sat up and nibbled on the chocolate. My face was damp with sweat.

"What did you see?"

I jumped at the sound of Theo's voice. I'd grown so used to only hearing him in my mind that hearing him out loud was foreign.

"T-Thaddeus," I stuttered. "He knows you're gone and he's mad. He was planning to use you to get me to come to him, I think. Now he has to come up with another plan. H-How did you get away?"

The others looked at Theo quizzically too. "Yeah, mate, surely they wouldn't have let you walk out and bit you adieu."

"I'll show you."

Theo closed his eyes and we all watched him. He held his hands up at his sides and then his form began to blur, like it was melting, then slowly began to fade into darkness.

A dark misty shadow took the place where Theo had stood. It became smaller and smaller until it was no bigger than an oddly shaped baseball. The shadow moved until it was beside me and then began to solidify.

Theo appeared beside me sitting on the couch with one foot resting on the opposite knee and his arm thrown over the couch behind me.

"Just like that."

"Whoa," Winston blurted, clearly impressed.

"I don't know of any protector that has the power to do such a thing," Ethan accused. "What are you?"

"My powers extend beyond most," Theo explained. "Mara is more special than you can comprehend, her duty to our world large, and therefore she needed a protector with powers this world hasn't seen before. I can do other things you wouldn't believe."

"Like what?" Adelaide asked.

He glanced at his sister. "Control minds."

"Is that how you were able to talk to me?" I blurted. "Because you could control my mind if you wanted?"

He shook his head. "I can't control yours—only speak to you. I couldn't *control* anyone here unless they meant you or me ill will. It's a recently acquired power of mine, if I'm being honest. I didn't find out about it until they took me. It kind of happened by accident," he muttered.

"How? What happened?" I probed, curious to know more.

He sighed, moving his damp hair out of his eyes. Now that I was feeling better I could tell he looked healthier than he had before. There was more color in his skin and there was a lightness to his eyes, though they quickly took on a haunted look as he opened his mouth to speak.

Nigel suddenly came running into the room from wherever he'd been hiding and jumped onto Theo's laugh.

"Nigel," he breathed, hiding his smile in the cat's fur as he hugged him.

I couldn't help but smile smugly since Theo had wanted me to leave the cat behind. I bet he was thankful now I'd insisted on escaping with him.

Still rubbing Nigel, he sat back and took a breath before launching into his story.

"They were interrogating me. They wanted me to tell them about you." His eyes flickered to me. "I wasn't going to tell them of course. But they kept at it, and at it, hitting me, cutting me, whatever they thought they could do to get me to talk. The next thing I knew I was inside the one guy's mind. It ... it was too much for him, and it'd never happened to me before, so when I escaped his mind and returned to my body he sorta ... evaporated."

"Like, poof?"

"Yeah." He nodded. "All that was left was this sort of vapor mist thing and then it was gone too. The other guy looked at me and fled from the room so fast."

"How badly did they hurt you?" I asked, my voice no more than a whisper.

"Nothing I can't handle, doll face." His lips quirked into a smile and he pulled me closer, placing a tender kiss on the side of my forehead. My eyes fluttered closed and I sighed happily.

"What did you learn when you were there?"

Theo released me and turned to Ethan who had spoken.

"Thaddeus is after Mara—we knew this, but ... he's almost insane with some need to have her. Mumbling to himself constantly. It seems like he's more focused on getting her than trying to control or hurt enchanters—I mean, he will if someone gets in his way, but ..."

"He wants me."

"Yeah," Theo sighed. "I followed him as a shadow most of the time, when I knew no one would be coming for me, and the guy is unhinged. He's mad. He wants to bring someone named Ganon back to life—but it's impossible. We have some wicked amazing powers but nothing can awaken the dead."

I felt suddenly bad I'd never thought about a spell to bring back Theo when I believed he was dead. I knew he said there *wasn't* one, but nonetheless I felt angry it hadn't occurred to me. I'd been too blindsided to think straight.

"How does Mara tie into this?" Ethan asked, his brow furrowed with worry.

Theo sighed. "Apparently, he needs something from Mara to bring this person back to life—or so he believes, because it's not possible."

Jee cleared his throat. "Unfortunately, it is."

All of our heads swiveled to him.

Jee's face grew shadowed and he bowed his head. "There is a very old, ancient spell, used to bring back the dead. It's only worked once, and … well, it wasn't exactly successful. The person who was brought back wasn't quite living, but wasn't dead, either."

"Like a zombie?" I interjected.

"Yes, I suppose, without the eating of the brains part." He stood and paced a few steps. "Thaddeus should be smart enough to know trying to bring back the dead isn't worth it. Unless …" He paused, tapping his lip and pacing some more.

"Unless?" Theo probed in a not very nice tone. I couldn't help but smile. Theo's smartass tone was one I was very familiar with.

"If he's trying to bring back your mother—he could, if he got the hair of her parents and the blood of her child. You." Jee looked straight at me, as did everyone else. "There are other ingredients needed of course, but those are easier to come by. Did you see her mother's body when you were there?" He directed the question to Theo.

"No." Theo shook his head. "But there was a room I was barred from. It was sheltered with some strong magic I couldn't penetrate."

"Ew, can you *not* use the word penetrate in a sentence?" Adelaide interjected.

Theo looked straight at her and enunciated, *"Penetrate."*

She shuddered and I stifled a laugh.

"I wouldn't put anything past someone like Thaddeus Lucero," Jee warned. "He was a powerful enchanter, one of the best, and turning to the Iniquitous would've only made him stronger. We have to stay vigilant. Especially when it comes to you." Jee's eyes met mine.

"Me?" I pointed to myself.

He nodded. "If Thaddeus wants you—he'll find a way to get you, mark my words."

chapter twenty

FTER THE EXCITEMENT OF THE day, I lay in bed staring up at the ceiling, with Adelaide snoring softly behind me.

Theo was back.

Thaddeus needed me.

And I hadn't told them about my brother—who he really wanted to bring back from the dead, if what he'd told me was true. He *was* an Iniquitous so he could always be lying.

I didn't have any explanation for why I *didn't* tell them. Something made me not want to.

My eyes fell to the clock on the nightstand. The bright green numbers blinked to tell me it was after two in the morning.

With a groan I slipped from the bed. Adelaide stirred and I hovered by the bed, waiting to move until I knew she was settled.

When I was sure she was actually asleep, I tiptoed from the room, out into the hall, and down the stairs.

"What are you doing up?" Theo's voice seemed loud and booming in the eerily quiet space. He was sitting up wide awake.

"I couldn't sleep."

He swung his feet to the floor and tipped his head at the now empty space beside him.

I settled into it, sitting so I could look at him.

For a moment neither of us said a word, only studied one another. It was our first moment truly alone since he'd reappeared.

He looked older, his eyes holding a darkness, which hadn't been there before. Theo had already been through a lot, but I was sure this experience was far worse.

Finally, I spoke. "I want you to know, it's okay if you're not okay."

He exhaled slowly, running his fingers through his overgrown dark hair.

"This life ... this is what I was born to do. It might not be easy, it's definitely dangerous, but I will never regret doing what it takes to protect you. You are my top priority."

"They could've killed you," I breathed, my voice cracking. "I thought they did."

"And I would've let them," he declared.

I swung my leg over, settling onto his lap so I was facing him.

His Adam's apple bobbed and his eyes flicked down to my lips.

"What are you doing, Mara?"

I curled my fingers into his hair and angled my face over his, our noses brushing together. His eyes closed and he let out the tiniest sigh. That sound made something in my belly stir. Having him there, this close, in a position we'd never been allowed before, excited me.

"What do you think I'm doing?" I whispered.

His hands settled on my hips, his fingers curling around my butt. His muscles strained like he wanted to push me away but couldn't bring himself to do it.

I could see the war still raged in him—the one that had been ingrained in him to push me away.

For once, he didn't say anything, which shocked me.

Maybe he was too tired to, or maybe he wanted this as badly as I did.

I pressed my lips softly to his, almost scared he might turn to smoke beneath me.

I didn't know what I'd do if he disappeared.

Life without him had been barely a life at all. To get him back and have him ripped away—I wasn't sure it was something I could recover from.

The pillow-light touch of my lips to his ignited a fire.

One second the kiss was soft, barely there, and the next we were grappling at one another like we were afraid the other was going to be ripped from our arms.

Tears coursed down my cheeks.

Tears of sadness, of fear, and of pure and utter relief because he was there.

He was real.

He was alive.

His heart beat steadily against me, a strong reminder of how he'd fought to get back to me.

I could never understand how our love was supposedly forbidden. Anything that felt like this needed to be shared, not smothered. He made me feel whole in a way I never had before. He was my missing piece, my other half, and now that I'd had him, lost him, and had him back again I was determined to never lose this again.

"Please don't cry for me," he murmured, pulling away. He brushed my tears away delicately like each one was precious and something to be cherished. "I don't deserve your tears."

"Of course you deserve them," I choked on a sob. "I love you—no one deserves them more than you."

He shook his head. "Loving me is too big of a burden. We were never meant to be together, and this is one of the reasons why. Your ... attachment to me can lead to you neglecting your duty."

"Theo," I argued, steel in my tone, "we don't even know what it is yet, so I can't exactly neglect it. And I refuse to allow you push me away now that I have you back. I thought you were *dead*. What if you'd spent six months thinking I was dead? Huh?"

His jaw clenched and I knew I had my answer.

"I don't care what rules there are or what other people say—you can't deny how right we are for each other." I took his hand and pressed it to my chest, over my heart before laying my own hand against his. "Do you feel that? Do you feel how they pulse together in sync? Some truths can't be denied and this is one of them. I was made to love you, and you were made to love me, and love ... it's the purest magic that exists, and you can't squander it once you find it."

With a growl, he crashed his lips to mine, kissing me with a bruising force. The metal of his lip ring stung my lip, but I didn't mind. He ravaged me with his kiss, almost like he was trying to punish me, or maybe himself, but he was failing miserable. I craved this rawness, the *realness*. This was us, always had been and always would be. We butted heads hard and loved harder. I wouldn't have it any other way. With Theo, I'd found my other half, and I wouldn't let him go easily.

He was stubborn.

But I could be worse.

I pushed my hands under his shirt, shoving it up and off.

My hands explored his chest and I stopped, his lips falling from mine.

"What?" he panted, out of breath.

My eyes followed the trail of my hands, stifling a sob.

"What did he *do* to you?" I pressed a shaking hand to my mouth, horrified by the sight in front of me.

He gathered my hands in his and forced me too meet his silvery gaze.

"He wanted to see how much pain he could inflict before I died. Fortunately, he never succeeded in his end goal."

Theo had always boasted tiny scars, from training over the years I assumed, but these were large gashes, still healing. They almost looked like claw marks. The skin was raw and red, clearly sore though he acted completely unbothered by my touch.

"I'm so sorry," I whispered. "I wish I could take your hurt away."

He kissed the palm of my hand and then held it to his chest. The bumps from the gashes felt like mountains on his skin.

"I would walk through hell and back for you. This … this is nothing."

Shaking, I couldn't stop thinking about healing him. He didn't deserve this pain. A blue light began to shimmer around my hand. Theo's lips parted as he watched, and my own mouth dropped open in awe as the skin around the cuts began to knit together and heal. Soon, nothing was left behind, not even a scar.

The blue light pulsed a few seconds longer before fading away.

Our eyes met in surprise and I remembered a long-ago conversation with Jessamine, one of my teachers, saying Chosen Ones could heal. I hadn't paid much mind to her, knowing she was half out of her mind, but right in front of me was the proof she wasn't lying. I'd healed Theo to the point not even one of the small scars from training remained behind. His skin was soft and smooth, as new as a baby's.

"That was ..."

"Strange?" I supplied.

He shook his head. "Wicked amazing." His tongue slid out suddenly, moistening his lips, and his eyes grew sad.

"What?" I prompted. "Theo?"

He shook his head, his Adam's apple bobbing. "I should stay far away from you. You're too good for me."

"Stop it," I growled out, my eyes full of fire. "Stop it right now. We are not going down this path again. I refuse. You will not push me away."

"He'll stop at nothing to get you," he confessed on a whisper. "Believe me, I know. He tried all kinds of ways to get the information out of me, but ..."

"But what?" I pleaded.

"My love for you was stronger than any sort of torture he could possibly think up."

"Exactly." I gripped his face between my hands, pressing my forehead to his. "That's why you can't deny what we have. It can't be wrong. I refuse to believe it."

He nodded slowly and I pressed my lips lightly to his. A tear fell down my cheek.

Theo was back.

He was here, in my arms, but our journey was only beginning and I feared I might lose him again, but for real this time.

chapter twenty-one

YOU'VE ONLY BEEN BACK A week and I swear you're trying to kill me," I panted at Theodore as he ran me through drills.

As much as we'd all been working together, and getting stronger, Theo demanded more. He was pushing us all to our breaking point. In the corner of the gym Winston was drenched in sweat, his hands on his hips, glaring at my boyfriend.

"You're a slave driver," he grumbled under his breath.

"I heard that, Churchill." Theo glanced in his direction raising a brow.

Winston grinned. "I meant for you to." Then he made a kissing face.

"I hate that guy," Theo growled softly to me.

I snickered. "Face it, you actually kind of like him."

Theo stood up straight. "I respect him. There's a difference. Now, get up off the floor and do it over again."

"Ugh," I groaned, but managed to lift my aching body up and into a standing position. Theo had me jumping over large blocks—I swore they had to be six feet tall, they were nearly as tall as Theo himself. But he insisted jumping over large obstacles would be beneficial in battle, so there we all were, jumping like maniacs. Poor Adelaide was so red in the face I feared she was seconds away from passing out. Maybe if she did he'd finally give us a break. The only person *not* subjected to this madness was Jee, not for lack of trying on Theo's part, though, but apparently even Theo didn't argue with Jee.

I pulled my white blond hair out of its ponytail and redid it, making sure to gather the shorter pieces that always wanted to come loose, before I started jumping again.

There was no way I was going to be able to get out of bed tomorrow, let alone do this again, and I hoped Theo knew that.

I believed he knew what he was talking about, he always seemed to be right, but that didn't mean I had to like it. My whole body felt like a wet stringy noodle.

I got a running start and launched my body over the block, falling on my ass on the other side.

Theo tilted his head, his arms crossed over his chest. "Again. Try landing on your feet this time. That's what they're for."

I glared at him. "And you try sleeping with one eye open tonight."

His lips twitched and I couldn't help but smile. At least I got him to break his stoic expression. Frankly, I couldn't stay mad at him too long. I'd missed him too much. I could even relish in him yelling at me like a drill sergeant because it meant he was here in front of me, flesh and blood.

I'd thought he was dead, and then he'd been only a voice in my mind, a ghost to me. But he hadn't left me. Our story wasn't over yet, and now I knew to cherish every moment.

I did it again and again and *again* before he finally gave me a break and went on to berating Winston and Ethan.

Adelaide sat on the floor stretching her legs out. She winced as she flexed her toes.

"Remind me again why I missed him?" she joked.

I bumped her shoulder with mine and we exchanged a smile. "Because he's your brother, and while he's hard headed, a giant pain in the ass, and an outright jerk most of the time, he really does love us."

"Yeah, he does," she sighed heavily. "But it's more tough love than sweet love." She stuck out her tongue.

"Heard that!" Theo called out.

"I meant for you to!" she retorted.

I shook my head. Those two were far more alike than either would ever admit.

Theo finished with Winston and Ethan and stood in the middle of the room surveying the four of us. "All right, two-mile cool down run and then we're done for the day."

"Theodore!" Adelaide scoffed. "Two miles is hardly a cool down! That's two freaking miles!"

He narrowed his gray eyes on her until they were nothing more than slits. "Want to make it four?"

"No, sir." She swallowed thickly and looked at me like a deer caught in headlights.

"Don't you think you're going a bit overboard?" I gave him a look.

That narrowed-eyed gaze landed on me next.

"All I'm saying is, you better run it with us."

He shook his head and grumbled out a, "Fine."

The five of us headed outside, Theo in the lead, to run two miles.

Those two miles felt like two hundred. I was already so sore from the day's exercises, not to mention the week of rigorous training Theo had already put us through. I thought we'd been working hard before, but that was a piece of cake compared to this. If we weren't prepared after this then we never would be.

When we left, Jee smirked at us, purposely walking by eating an ice cream sundae. After all this I'd be too tired to eat anything. I wasn't sure I could even get in the shower.

As our two mile "cool down" came to an end, the four of us stumbled inside Jee's building while Theo remained bright as a daisy. I might kick him in the shin later for the hell of it. That arrogant smirk of his was getting to me. He was lucky he was so handsome.

Once inside we all took turns showering. Mine took forever since I could barely lift my arms to wash my hair and, as sweaty as it was, there was no way I couldn't *not* wash it. Theo owed me a full body massage after all this with *no* fun times for him.

I dried off my body and hair as best I could with the towel before gathering it up in a messy bun. It was getting really long and I should probably cut it so it wouldn't get in my way, but I kind of liked it. For now I wouldn't worry about it.

I changed into a loose pair of shorts and a t-shirt. Something comfy, but I wouldn't look like a total bum. I glanced at my reflection in the mirror. Scratch that, I looked like a bum, but I didn't care.

I slowly made my way downstairs, wincing with every step as it sent a spasm up my legs. I'd woken up three times the night before with cramps in my legs. Something told me I'd be up even more tonight.

Something delicious smelling hit my nose and I perked up as my belly came to life. I hadn't been sure I could eat, especially when I thought I'd have to make something myself, but my stomach had other ideas.

"We have pizza!" Adelaide called from where she sat on the floor. Several pizza boxes were open on the coffee table.

"I thought you guys deserved it." Theo shrugged, picking up a slice and leaning back in a chair to eat it. How the hell did he make eating a pizza look sexy?

I grabbed a napkin and a slice of pizza before sitting down on the floor beside Theo's chair. He looked down at me with a small smile, his leg brushing my arm. We both felt the need to stay close to each other. I was scared if he was out of my sight for too long he'd disappear completely. I ate my piece of pizza slowly, not only savoring it but also wanting to make sure the greasy goodness wasn't too much for my stomach.

Finishing the one I started another but could only eat half. Theo grabbed the uneaten half from my hand before I could toss it and ate it, grinning down at me like the Cheshire cat.

It was all so normal.

In the middle of all this craziness, when a war was brewing, somehow we could find this little piece of heaven all to ourselves. It was such a simple thing, hanging out eating pizza with your friends, with the love of your life, but when only a week ago you thought you'd never have this again, it becomes everything.

Adelaide wiped her fingers on a napkin. "So, when exactly are we going after this fucker? No one messes with my brother and gets away with it."

"Adelaide," I snorted.

"What?" She shrugged daintily, her motions totally at odds with her previous statement.

Theo chuckled. "I don't know, but I applaud your enthusiasm. I didn't know you had it in you."

She tossed a pillow at his head. "Ass hat, I watched you be, what I thought at the time, murdered. But instead you've been held hostage by a psychopath Iniquitous for *months*. Excuse me if I have some pent-up rage I need to unleash."

"We have to be smart about this," Theo said, smacking his hands together heatedly. "We can't be unprepared like last time."

"We can't lose anyone this time either," I whispered softly. I knew this was probably a futile hope, in a war there are casualties, but I couldn't help but put it out there. "We have to stick together."

"I agree." Adelaide stuck her chin in the air haughtily.

Theo shook his head but said nothing. He knew, as did we all, this was unlikely. It was easier to pretend everyone in this room would get to live a long life.

I stood and gathered up all the trash and empty boxes. Despite the soreness in my body I suddenly needed something to do. I didn't want to think about the reality of living without any of these people. I'd only known them a year, but they were my family. Besides, I'd already lost Theo once. I wasn't sure I was strong enough to survive losing him again.

Before I could finish cleaning up everything, Theo pulled me down and into his lap.

I let out a small laugh. "Hi."

"Hey." He nuzzled my neck and I warmed beneath his touch. I smiled and kissed his cheek. It was weird almost, being out in the open with him like this. Before, at the manor, all our moments had been stolen, secret, only for us. But here, we didn't have to worry.

He rubbed his thumb in soothing circles against my back where my shirt had ridden up.

"Bleh," Adelaide pretended to gag from her spot on the floor. "You two are sickeningly sweet and I can't handle it. Get a room."

"Offering yours?" Theo teased.

Her eyes widened. "No, no, absolutely *not*. Do not even think about fornicating in my room."

Now I was the one fake gagging. "Oh, my God Adelaide, could you like *not* talk about your brother and me that way."

She blushed. "Oh, God, I'm imagining it now. Make it go away. Why did I do this to myself?" She squealed, rubbing her eyes like it could erase the mental image she'd conjured up for herself.

"Here, love," Winston said and grabbed her face between his hands. Her eyes opened briefly, but only for a second, before he kissed her. Not a soft peck on the lips, either. No, this was a full-blown make out kiss.

Theo growled. "Get off my sister."

After a few more seconds, he let her go.

"What are you thinking about now?" he asked her, completely ignoring the daggers Theo was staring into the back of his skull.

"That."

He grinned triumphantly at having accomplished his mission.

"Try that again in front of me, Churchill, and you won't live long enough to see the next dawn."

Winston stared back at Theo, completely unbothered. "Is it so completely abhorrent to you to think I might actually *like* your sister and she might like me back?"

"Wait ... you like me?" Adelaide asked in a small voice, pointing to herself.

Winston grinned at her. "Well, yeah, I think it's pretty obvious, or at least it should be now."

Her cheeks tinged pink and in a move which shocked us all she grabbed his shirt in her fist and yanked him to her, kissing him even more passionately than he had only seconds before.

Theo growled in my ear. "Down, boy," I warned him. "Let them be happy."

He rolled his eyes at me and let out a sigh that sounded strangely like *not happening.* I elbowed him in the ribs and his next sigh sounded a lot like an agreement.

When the kiss broke I eyed Theo and he bit out a gruff, "I'm happy for you guys."

"Don't lie, Theodore," Adelaide snorted. "It looks stupid on you."

"See?" He turned to me. "No point in making me lie they know I don't approve *but* ..." His face softened as he looked at his baby sister. "I will do my best to be happy for you because all I want is *you* to be happy."

Adelaide laid her head on Winston's chest. "And he makes me happy. Thanks, Theodore."

I smiled at Theo and kissed him, letting him know without words that for once I approved of his behavior.

He smiled back at me, brushing a piece of hair behind my ear which had fallen loose from my bun. I captured his hand in mine before he could let it drop, entwining our fingers together. I looked down at our joined hands and felt a tug in my heart, like it recognized the feel of his hand and was saying *mine*.

chapter twenty-two

"CAN YOU TELL ME AGAIN *exactly* what she said?" Theo prodded as the two of us sat on the floor of the living room in the middle of the night long after all the others had gone to sleep. We weren't purposely being secretive. The nighttime was the only time we could really be alone together, and instead of sexy times most of the time we went over every detail we knew that might help us in our quest to defeat Thaddeus.

Once again, I went over in great detail our meeting with Cleo, telling him about how she said we were soul bound, and about the key.

"Where's the key?" he asked.

I pulled out the chain containing the firefly necklace from him, the key now hanging beside the jar.

He smirked. "Smart girl. Now tell it all to me again."

"Theodore," I groaned, ready to smack him upside the head. "We've been over this ten times already. I don't know what else I could possibly tell you that I haven't."

He rolled his eyes. "This is important. Cleo is ancient. She doesn't just talk to anybody. Meeting her wasn't a coincidence."

I took a deep breath. "Fine, let me try something."

I closed my eyes and twisted my neck. Reaching up, I placed my hands on his face.

"Uh ... Mara?"

"Shut up," I seethed. "I need to concentrate."

I wasn't sure if what I was trying was even possible, but I figured with our combined freaky special powers it might work.

I hoped.

Behind my closed lids, colors began to swirl and transform.

"What's happening?" Theo's voiced was laced with panic.

"Shh, trust me."

I felt his body relax beneath my hands as the picture became clearer and through my eyes he watched the entire conversation with Cleo play out. It was interesting for me too to watch it like this, not in the moment and able to entirely observe it.

"Jee," she hissed under her breath, "why are you here?"

"I brought friends," he explained.

"I can see that ... well not see, but I know," she griped.

"We—they—need to talk to you. It's important."

"Well, I don't want to talk to them." She turned away, giving us her shoulder.

I opened my mouth to argue but Jee gave me a look, silencing me.

"Cleo," he said in a sickly sweet voice, "this is important."

"You've said that once already—twice is just repetitive. I'm blind not stupid."

"I never ask you for anything, do I, Cleo?"

Watching now I could sense her unease. Her wariness of magical strangers. I didn't quite understand what she was exactly, some oracle of some sort I assumed, but it was clear she'd been mistreated in the past.

"I'm asking for your help now. For my friends. You know I wouldn't be here if it wasn't necessary."

She swiveled back to face us. "I'm not in the habit of giving favors but I suppose this once I can make an exception." I watched as she looked at each of us. She was blind but yet in some way she could clearly see each of us. How fascinating.

"*Thank you.*" Jee bent and placed a kiss on her cheek.

"*Very well,*" she muttered. "*Let's not do this out in the open.*"

She placed a closed sign on her cart and stood.

"*Follow me.*"

She led us through the mall, and down a hallway, through a door and then another before we were in a storage closet. Once the door closed behind us and it was dark she tapped her cane against the cement wall three times in a triangle pattern. The wall melted away and we stepped into her home.

"*Welcome to my humble abode.*" She sunk onto one of the cushions. "*Sit, sit.*"

We all did, and ended up in a circle with her in the center.

"*So, tell me light one, why are you here?*"

"*Why do people call me that?*"

"*Light one, dark one, it's all about the balance really. The balance can't be disrupted without everything going ... Well, let's just say it'd be bad.*"

"*Dark one,*" I repeated softly. "*That's what the Iniquitous called Theo before ... before ...*"

She smiled, flicking her fingers so hundred of candles littered around the room sprung to life.

"*You cannot have the light without the dark. It's all about balance. When the fates align and connect you get two halves of a whole.*"

218

Winston cleared his throat. "Are you saying Mara and Theo are soul bound?"

"Soul bound?" I repeated. "What is that?"

Her lips twitched. "It's when the cosmos create a soul too great, too powerful, for one body to sustain it so they break it apart, and two separate souls are born, but they are in fact one."

"This doesn't mean we're like brother and sister, right?"

"No." She laughed like I was silly. "It means you're connected in a ways most only dream of."

"Like not even death could separate us?"

She frowned. "Yes, not even death could cross such barriers."

"That's not why we came here."

"I assumed not." She clasped her hands and laid them in her lap.

"When we were fleeing the manor in Seattle, we found Victor. I don't know if you know him—"

"Antonescu?"

"Yes, that's him."

"Continue."

I took a breath. "He was dying, and he told me I had to get away from there and I had to find Cleo. That she—you—held the key to the truth. But I don't know what that is. What's the truth, Cleo?"

Her lips twitched with a slight smile. "I knew you'd come to me one day. Your mother knew too."

"My mother? How do you know my mother? You're my age, right?"

Jee shook his head and laughed.

"Looks can be deceiving, Mara." She pulled her lips back revealing her teeth, the incisors sharpened to fangs. "I've walked this earth longer than anyone should. It's a lonely life—a half life—but it's my life."

She smoothed her hands over her skirt and looked at me.

"I should warn you, child, the truth is not always easy to accept. Sometimes the truth seems like another lie. Truth is a sword. It cuts you and rips out parts of you that you didn't even know you had. But alas, you're here, like the stars foretold, and therefore I'll give it to you."

She stood and walked over to the far wall, fiddling on a bookshelf. She picked up several books looking inside before shelving them. Finally, she pulled out an emerald green one with a leather bookmark attached and found what she was looking for.

She clasped a small object in her hand and walked over to me.

Opening her hand, she held out to me.

"The key." She shook her hand. "Take it."

"What's it for?" I asked, looking up at her.

"That, I cannot tell you. You will know when the time comes."

"Uh ... thanks, I guess."

She laughed. "It'll all make sense in due time."

"May I?" Cleo asked.

I nodded.

She clasped my necklace and her eyes rolled back in her head. I almost jerked away from her, but somehow I held still. She let go and smiled at me, her fangs poking into her bottom lip.

"Oh, it is exactly as the stars have told me. The darkness cowers. I shall celebrate."

Just like it began, the memory swirled in color and then I opened my eyes to look at Theo. Slowly, he blinked his eyes open, the pupils dilated.

"How did you do that?" he breathed, his eyes wide with wonder.

I shook my head. "I'm not sure. I thought I might be able to show you, since we're connected, but I didn't think it would actually work."

He took my hand in his flipping it palm up and tracing the lines in it. "You amaze me," he whispered so softly I wasn't sure if he actually meant for me to hear so I didn't respond. He looked up at me flicking his dark hair out of his eyes. "There seems to be no limit to what you can do. It blows my mind. I feel like I should bow before my Queen."

I snorted. "No bowing, please."

He grinned, his eyes flickering with light. "I don't plan on it, but if I was to kneel it would only be before you."

I cupped his face in one hand. I didn't say anything for a moment, just felt the pulses of his body beneath my hand. "We have a long road ahead of us."

"We do," he agreed, placing his hand over top of mine. "But together, we'll overcome it."

"You mean it? You're not going to go rogue and abandon me because you think it's for my own good?"

He chuckled huskily. "If I actually thought it'd be for your good I would—but I know we're stronger together."

"I love you," I whispered.

"God, I love you too," he murmured back. "I don't know what I did to deserve you, but whatever it is I'm glad for it."

He leaned forward and kissed me slowly, softly. It was a simple kiss but somehow I still felt it all the way down to my toes. Every time he touched me I felt it everywhere. Little tiny zings of electricity made my body hum.

His body pressed into mine, urging me to lie back on the floor. He kissed me deeper, the cool metal of his lip ring a stark contrast to the heat of his lips. A small moan escaped me and he captured it with a soft chuckle. My body warmed, not only from the feel of his body but from the electricity created between us. I was slowly being set on fire, but he made it a pleasant experience.

My hands delved into his hair and he captured them, entwining his fingers with mine before pinning my hands above my head.

"Theo," I panted between kisses. "Let me touch you."

"No," he growled hungrily. "This is my time."

This is my time.

Oh, my God, I might spontaneously combust.

The kiss reached scorching levels and I writhed beneath him, pressing my hips up and into his, begging silently for more.

We'd only had sex the one time, and it felt like so long ago. I needed to feel him against him more than I needed my next breath.

He broke the kiss long enough to place a soft kiss to my neck and whisper, "You make me crazy."

"The feeling is mutual."

He smashed his lips to mine and I moaned again, unable to quiet myself. I should've probably been embarrassed by all the sounds I was making, and the fact we were on the floor in the living room, but I needed him so badly I couldn't bring myself to care in the moment.

Tomorrow, I'd probably hate myself, but for now this took precedence over any potential embarrassment.

His fingers crept slowly under my sleep shirt and I shivered as goose bumps suddenly dotted my skin. It didn't matter what he did, my body reacted immediately like I was a puppet and he was my master. I felt the brush of his fingers on the underside of my breast and I gasped, my hips rising against his.

"Theo," I breathed.

"No bra?" he joked.

"I'm in my pajamas, dick wad."

He laughed warmly and kissed my lips, then my neck, before taking his other hand and with one finger pulling my t-shirt down into a V shape so he could kiss the top curve of each breast.

I should have told him to stop, not here, this wasn't the place for this, but I couldn't find the words because I wanted him more than I wanted to be responsible.

Since my hands were finally free to wander I grabbed the hem of his shirt, edging it up. He sat up, leaving enough space between us for him to remove it.

I bit my lip, gliding my hands down his chest and abs, his skin smooth and flawless now. I'd loved it before, and I still loved it, but somehow unscarred it seemed less Theo.

He lowered again, kissing me deeply like he couldn't get enough of me.

It was amazing how with one touch, one kiss, he could make me feel so loved. There was no questioning how he felt about me, how we felt about each other. It was there, written as plainly as words in the touches and gestures and even the glances.

There was something so amazing about a love so undeniable.

It was rare, it was special, the kind of magic that exists freely in the world but, so few ever find it.

Slowly, like unwrapping a present we took turns removing the rest of our clothes.

When we finally joined, I swore lights sparkled around us.

I nearly wept with joy at being connected like this once more with him, but I dammed down the tears knowing Theo would love to pick on me later.

He nuzzled his face against my neck, his lips resting at the point where my pulse jumped in time with every erratic heartbeat.

He glided one of his hands through my hair to rest at the nape of my neck, bringing my head forward until our foreheads were pressed against each other.

"Do you feel that?" he murmured. "The way we're made for one another?"

I nodded. I did. I'd felt it long before I ever wanted to admit and wanted to keep believing he was nothing more than my asshat protector.

But Theo was more. He'd always been so much more to me.

I crashed my lips to his, wrapping my arms around his neck. I couldn't get close enough to him. He kissed me back with just as much passion and I soaked it up like a flower who'd been without the sun. I guess that was a pretty accurate description of Theo and me. We were both dependent on each other in order for the other to survive.

The thick scruff on his cheeks was rough beneath my palms but I'd never tell him to shave it. I loved how it somehow made him even more handsome, ruggedly so.

"I love you," he whispered once more.

I gasped, suddenly unable to find the words, but he knew. He always knew.

***

It was early in the morning, light would soon be creeping in the windows, and we lay curled on the floor, wrapped in a blanket and each other's arms. We should have gotten up and put our clothes on, and I should have returned to the room I shared with Adelaide, but for the moment we were both content to stay there.

Theo glided his fingers through my hair absentmindedly, like this was something he did all the time. I drew random shapes on his bare chest, watching the slight pulses in his skin from the beat of his heart and each breath he took.

I knew it wasn't realistic, but I wished I could pause this moment and live there forever. The peace, the quiet, his arms around me, it was all so perfect.

I saw a drop of water appear on his chest and I startled, realizing I was crying.

"What's wrong?" he whispered into the dark, his fingers stilling in my hair. "Did I hurt you?" He started to sit up but I shook my head.

"No, no," I hastened to calm him. "I don't know why I'm crying. I guess, because this is so nice. It was barely the blink of an eye ago when I thought you were dead.

That this would never happen again. I realize now I was barely getting by—how difficult it was without you."

"You need me," he stated with a grin.

I laughed softly. "Yeah, I do."

I'd proven I could survive without him, but it wasn't the same. Life without Theo was black and white. He brought color and vibrancy to my life. Without him I had no anchor. I was a boat adrift at sea. Now that he was back my life was exploding with brilliance once more, there was only one major problem.

Thaddeus.

I had to kill him.

I knew it as sure as I knew I loved Theo or that I was going to take my next breath. This world, mine, ours, the enchanted and the human, depended on his dying.

They say good and bad must coexist side by side for balance, it might be true, but evil had no place anywhere and Thaddeus was pure evil. He'd kill every last enchanter to get what he wanted, and in the end he still wouldn't be satisfied.

chapter twenty-three

"THIS IS SO FUN!" Adelaide squealed, her hand clasped in Winston's and in the other a large bucket of popcorn held closely to her chest. "It's like we're normal humans!"

"Shh!" I hushed her, paying for the popcorn, box of chocolate, sour gummy bears, and two drinks for Theo and myself. Theo had already grabbed our large popcorn bucket and was piling even more oily butter into it. I wasn't going to complain though. Greasy movie theater butter was part of the reason anybody came to the movies.

Theo, Ethan, and Jee had discussed it and after some minor preparation and talks on what to do in an emergency—like we get attacked in the middle of a movie theater, which seemed highly unlikely to me—

they agreed all of us could go see a movie to get out for a while.

Frankly, it was a break we all very much needed. So even if they had spent all of yesterday going over *What do in case of ...* plans, I wasn't going to complain and nobody else was, either.

In front of me, Winston and Adelaide disappeared into the darkened theater. We'd all agreed to see a comedy—deciding our life was already enough of a horror show and action packed. Adelaide and I would've loved to see a romantic movie, but the guys out voted us, so comedy it was.

Theo fell into step beside me, Jee and Ethan were behind us.

"This is so good," he said around a mouthful of popcorn, already helping himself.

I laughed. "Try and save some for me, would ya?"

"No promises." He winked.

My heart warmed, for a moment pretending I'd never learned I was an enchanter, and we were a normal human couple enjoying a simple date at the movies.

Inside the screening room the lights were dimmed. Adelaide and Winston headed for the seats nearest the emergency exit, like we'd already discussed. I hated we had to look over our shoulders, as if each of our breaths was a countdown to the last—a ticking time bomb waiting for the right second to implode.

The six of us lined up in a row. There was still about twenty minutes before the show started. The guys wanted time to scan the perimeter of the building and clear the nearby buildings before letting us in. They took this whole security thing super seriously. After all this was over, if it ever ended that was, they should think about protecting the President's daughter or something.

God, what if this never did end?

Would we have to live our life like this every day until we died? Always looking over our shoulder, and second-guessing every look from a stranger? Theo and I weren't even ready for this, let alone had we discussed it, but would we ever be free to marry and have children? Once upon a time I dreamt of going to college, meeting my future husband, and settling down and having some kids. It sounded peaceful and wonderful.

Now, all that seemed like some little girl's fairy tale wish. Something so silly and far fetched it could never possibly come true.

I pushed those thoughts out of my mind, refusing to dwell on things like that when there were far more important things for me to worry about. For now, I was going to focus on enjoying myself. Moments like those were fleeting.

I placed Theo's cup in the holder beside him and did the same with mine. He held the popcorn bucket hostage in his lap, so I held onto the chocolate—Reese's Pieces and M & M's—and sour gummy worms.

I opened the sour gummy worm pack first and popped one in my mouth. My taste buds danced across my tongue at the tartness.

"If you eat all that popcorn *you're* going to get the refill," I warned him.

He merely looked at me and shrugged. "Okay."

"Maybe I should've gotten my own."

"Maybe." He shoved another handful in his mouth.

"Here, take this." I deposited my snacks into Jee's lap beside me. Before he could protest I was up and heading out to the concession stand for my own popcorn.

"Mara, wait," Theo groaned behind me. His protector mojo was raging strong and refusing to let me get away from him.

He caught up to me quickly, grumbling about girls, sensitive, and that he was *going* to share.

We both knew it was a lie. He could eat enough to feed fifty people and still go back for seconds and maybe thirds.

Since I wasn't going to be sharing with anyone I got a smaller bucket, one which couldn't fit two people's hands inside of it, and went over to the counter to add more butter into it. I inhaled the scent of fake movie theater butter, smiling to myself. Leave it to greasy artificial food to make me feel better.

Armed with my own bucket of popcorn we headed into the theater once more.

I took my candy back from Jee and eyed him shrewdly. "There better not be any gummy worms or chocolate missing."

He cracked a grin. "I don't want your PMS candy."

I stuck my tongue out at him.

A few minutes later the lights turned dark and the screen flickered to life with previews. Adelaide made an excited squeal that sounded like a baby pig.

This was the first time she'd ever been to the movies, same for Theo, and maybe for the others too. It wasn't something I'd done often before, but Dani and I had gone some.

Dani ... the girl who'd been there for me practically my entire life. The one I felt like I'd abandoned. I didn't know how she was, or if she was safe, and unfortunately contact was not possible. If she was safe and the Iniquitous didn't know about her I had to keep it that way. I couldn't risk any contact back home for fear of bringing harm to any of them. Enough damage had already been dealt the night I left.

Theo's hand suddenly entwined with mine and he gave it a small squeeze. Somehow, freaking protector powers, or our connection, he'd sensed me growing upset.

I flashed him a grateful smile, though I couldn't be positive he'd seen it in the dark theater.

I wiggled in the seat and focused on eating my snacks and waited for the previews to end and for the movie to begin.

***

Emerging from the theater into the bright afternoon sunlight was like having your retinas personally victimized by the sun.

"My eyes!" Adelaide cried, slapping a hand over them. "My poor eyes!"

We all stood on the sidewalk for a moment letting our eyes adjust to the brightness.

After a minute, Adelaide spoke again. "Do we have to go back to the apartment yet?"

Jee scoffed. "What's wrong with my apartment?"

She turned her gaze to him. "Nothing—except it's pretty much a prison."

He shrugged, unable to argue with her words.

Theo twisted his lips, thinking. "We've got a few hours until the sun starts going down, so I don't see why not."

"Thank you!" Adelaide cried and jumped into his arms.

He chuckled and hugged her back before setting her down.

We were in downtown Minneapolis so there were plenty of shops and restaurants we could get to on foot, though we had brought the car in case we needed a faster escape.

"On one condition, though," Theo warned, pointing a finger at her. "We all have to stick together."

She rolled her eyes. "Like I expected you to say we could separate."

He grinned. "I'm glad you know me so well."

"Enough standing here, let's *go*." She grabbed Winston's hand and started dragging him down the street, leaving the rest of us to follow.

Theo slipped his hand in mine as we walked and I looked down, smiling at the ease with which he did it. Theo had had far more trouble easing into our relationship than I had—granted I hadn't been raised being told I wasn't allowed to fall in love with my protector, whereas he'd always been told a relationship was forbidden between us.

The six of us were relatively ignored by passersby as we wandered around, even with Adelaide squealing at every little thing.

I wasn't really interested in looking or shopping. Instead, I enjoyed the feel of the sun on my skin and being with my friends.

After going into a few shops we decided to get dinner before heading back to the apartment. I could tell Theo was getting antsy but it wasn't even dark yet when we made it back to the apartment. He was as much a worrier as he was a literal warrior.

I guess having had enough time with each other we all went our separate ways. Theo and I found ourselves alone in the training room. More often than not we were hanging out in there. It was one of the few places everyone else avoided unless they had to be there.

We lay on the floor side by side staring up at the ceiling. So long ago it felt we'd done the same thing, me in a pretty dress, him in a tux, with thousands of teal fireflies swarming around us. Now the green of the garden was replaced with gray walls and the grass beneath was nothing but a cushy mat.

Theo must've been thinking of the same memory as me because suddenly he swirled his hand in the air and the beautiful fireflies appeared. The one in my little jar necklace fluttered faster, trying to get out.

"Sometimes I miss it—the manor," I admitted. "Especially the garden and our library."

He turned to face me, his arms crossed behind his head. "Me too. Those were the only places I didn't have to worry about how I looked at you."

I rolled to my side and reached out, tracing my finger over his lips. "And how did you look at me?"

"Like I loved you."

"And do you? Love me?"

He nipped lightly at my finger. "You know I do."

"Say it," I pleaded. I would never get sick of hearing those words on his lips.

"I love you," he murmured.

"And I love you."

I squeaked in surprise when I suddenly found myself on my back with him above me.

"Despite your pig headedness, I love you." He kissed my neck.

"Oh, I'm the pig headed one, am I?" I joked and he silenced my laughter with a kiss to my lips.

"Even when you back talk me somehow I love you more." He kissed my left cheek.

"When you defy my orders, I still love you." This time he kissed my forehead.

"I love everything about you. Forever and always."

"Forever and always," I echoed.

chapter twenty-four

Y OU KNOW THAT FEELING WHEN things are going good, maybe too good, and you know it can't last forever?

That's how I was feeling.

I wasn't sure if the others sensed it but I felt as if a ticking time bomb was counting down before a major explosion left us in dust.

We'd made it to August with no signs of the Iniquitous and no more dreams about Thaddeus on my end. To me it was as if they'd gone quiet, dormant maybe, waiting and biding their time so when they struck they'd get exactly what they wanted.

With September quickly approaching, though, I doubted we had much time left.

It'd been last Christmas when Thaddeus had made his attempt to get me.

Something told me he wouldn't let a whole year pass without trying again.

But this time we'd be prepared. We had to be.

I scaled the rope Theo had installed in the gym in seconds, dinging the bell at the top. When he first put it up I couldn't haul myself up three feet let alone all the way up. I made my way back down slowly, having learned the hard way about rope burn. I didn't stop when my feet hit the floor, though. Oh no, Theo had set up a whole freaking obstacle course, not just in the gym but through the entire house and everyone, even Jee, was being subjected to it and timed. Whoever did it the fastest didn't even win anything, except bragging rights.

"This is the stupidest God damn thing I've ever done in my entire existence," Jee heaved out the words with each heavy breath he took as he tried to haul his body over top of a large block. He made it and then rolled right on the other side landing face first on the floor.

I didn't pause to help, though I should I supposed, because again this was *timed* and I knew Theo would give me hell if I wasn't the fastest.

I jumped over the hurdles he'd set up—they were even taller than normal hurdles used in track, so all the jumping training he'd put me through really helped here.

Then I had to scale the rock wall to the top, and go all the way over to the right before coming back down again.

Normally, my muscles would be *screaming* at me in protest by now, but months of vigorous activities had sharpened not only my skills but increased my endurance. I felt sure if we had to leave on foot I could run a marathon distance before I had to stop. I was proud of how far I'd come but it'd been *hard* work and hadn't happened over night. In fact, I wasn't even sure when some of this stuff went from feeling impossible to easy. I guess that's the thing about progress, it happens so slowly you don't even notice it.

From the rock wall I had "buildings" to scale, which were basically tall wooden walls Theo had built himself—no idea when he had time to do that. His reasoning for those was, if we had to get away quickly we could always go *up* that way if we were out we wouldn't have to worry about being cornered in an alleyway. Seriously, he'd thought of everything. I wasn't sure when he slept. All he seemed to think about was preparing us for different possibilities. We hadn't talked about it much but I had a feeling that night at the manor, when he sacrificed himself, haunted him. Knowing Theo he'd obsessed over everything he could've and should've done differently. What he seemed to forget was, the manor should've been a safe place. They should've never known about it. He couldn't control that, but Theo? He always had to feel like he was in control of the situation.

I scaled up the wooden wall, landing on a solid surface. Jesus, he'd even built a makeshift roof so that it'd be like running on top of a building.

I ran across and climbed down the other side. I wasn't sure what to call what he'd set up next, but I had to drop down and crawl under it.

"This is ridiculous," I grumbled.

I made it through and had to then climb some sort of netting. After, the course took me out of the gym where he'd set up the magical portion of the test. How he'd gotten Jee to agree to let him do this part in his apartment was beyond me, but I'd learned by now that what Theo wanted he got.

I blasted through those so easily I could hear Jee cursing somewhere behind me about not burning down his house. Rolling my eyes, I kept going.

My power came so easily and effortlessly to me now that sometimes I wondered why I ever struggled in controlling it. Once you got the hang of it, it was as natural as breathing, such an engrained part of me I didn't even have to think to control it half the time.

The course came to a stop in front of Theo leaning against the kitchen counter with a stopwatch.

"Time," he called, when I crossed the piece of blue tape on the floor.

I joined Ethan and Winston who were already done. We'd each started several minutes apart so the course didn't clog with us fighting. We wouldn't find out who was fastest until the end.

Jee finished a few minutes after me, having caught up on the magical portion of the test.

Last was Adelaide. She'd improved a lot that was for sure, I was seriously proud of her, and I knew she could pull this off if she didn't psych herself out. She always seemed to underestimate herself, and I felt bad because yeah, she was behind the rest of us but we'd all been training longer—even me since Theo had given me private lessons at the manor. It wasn't her fault and she was catching up quick. I knew she was a force to be reckoned with but *she* didn't know it yet. She'd know it soon enough, though.

Red-faced and sweating Adelaide finished, her wild curly hair had escaped the confines of the elastic ponytail holder refusing to be tamed.

Theo recorded his time on his trusty clipboard. He looked like a track coach or something. I was surprised he didn't have a whistle and baseball cap on to really capture the essence of his persona.

"Who came in first?" I was the first to ask, despite the fact we were all impatiently waiting. Even Jee, who tapped his foot sharply against the floor.

Theo looked up from his clipboard. "Is it really that important?"

"Yes," we all echoed through the cavernous room.

He sighed and shoved the fingers of one hand through his hair.

"Ethan's first."

"Yes," Ethan cried, raising his arms in the air in triumph.

"Mara second."

I nodded, pleased. First place would've been best, of course, but second wasn't bad.

"Winston third."

I held my breath.

"Adelaide fourth."

Adelaide let out an ear-piercing shriek I was positive reverberated through the entire city and counties beyond.

"I came in *fourth?*" she asked, tears shimmering in her eyes.

I was certain that in the history of forever no one had ever been happier to come in *fourth* place than Adelaide Meyers in that moment.

Theo snorted. "Um, yeah ... and that leaves Jee in fifth."

Jee rolled his eyes. "This thing is rigged."

Theo narrowed his eyes. "Are you suggesting I'm bias?" Jee opened his mouth but before he could respond Theo continued, "Because if I was then Churchill here wouldn't have finished at all."

"Hey," Winston protested, wounded.

Theo's eyes shot to him. "You play tonsil hockey with my sister. If I hated you before I detest you now."

Winston shrugged, the gesture saying *fair enough.*

Winston slung one arm over Adelaide's shoulders and bent to kiss her cheek.

Theo bristled a small growl rumbling in his chest.

I moved toward him and wrapped my arm around his waist. "Down, boy."

He mumbled something under his breath I couldn't catch.

There was protective and then there was Theodore. He was a *whole* other level. I think the word for it was *crazy*. But I'd never tell him that.

At our feet, Nigel circled around us. Theo bent and picked him up, the Russian Blue nuzzling into his neck.

"All right hit the showers I guess," he announced.

I snorted, stepping away from him. "What are you, our football coach now? Hit the showers?" I mocked.

"I don't even know what football is so I don't know if I should be offended or not."

I laughed and shook my head. "No need to be offended."

As the others headed off I grabbed a protein bar from the kitchen and hopped up on the counter. Theo joined me, placing his hands on either side of my hips.

Tilting his head he regarded me. "You did good."

I mock gasped. "Is *the* Theodore actually complimenting little ole me?"

He pinched my cheek mockingly. "Don't get used to it."

I took a bite of my bar. "No, no, don't backtrack on me now. I want to hear all about how wonderful I am. Best girlfriend ever, right?"

"Ever?" He raised a brow.

I shoved his chest playfully. "I mean, I did pine for you when I thought you were dead."

He dipped his head, cracking a smile. "Yep, and you would've never ever moved on. I'm too wonderful to ever get over."

I frowned. "You're right," I said seriously.

There was no way under the sun I would've ever moved on from Theodore. Without him I would've lived the rest of my life alone. At that point our love story might've been short, but it was epic, it wasn't something that could be replicated. The feeling was too unique. A love that special can't be replicated, so why bother? It wouldn't have been about punishing myself into being alone, it would've been me accepting that no one else would ever be Theodore. It wouldn't have been fair to any potential guy out there to try to love him because nothing would ever come close to this feeling.

He stared into my eyes. "I wouldn't have been mad, you know—if you moved on. You shouldn't be alone the rest of your life if I'm gone."

I chewed the last of my bar and laid the wrapper on the counter before twinning my arms around his neck. "No one would ever be *you*, Theo, and wouldn't be fair to them because I would always love you *more*."

He didn't say anything. Instead, he kissed me, and that kiss ...

It said it all.

chapter twenty-five

I SAT IN FRONT OF THE window and watched the
multi-colored leaves swirl to the ground.

In Minnesota, when summer ended, the
temperatures seemed to immediately drop.
Something told me winter would be coming early.

I'd always loved fall though. The colors of the
leaves, the coolness in the air, the way the ground
crunched beneath the soles of my shoes, coffee and
cider, blankets and sweatshirts. There wasn't anything
I didn't love about it.

But this year, I couldn't seem to enjoy it like I
normally did. Not when I knew the evil that was out
there, thriving, breathing just as we did. They needed to
be eradicated like a deadly disease, because that's
essentially what they were.

Maybe I shouldn't have been so focused on vengeance.

But I didn't feel like I had a vendetta. I only wanted to protect my people. All those enchanters who'd been slaughtered in the manor and at the New York safe house too. They didn't deserve to die in such a way. It was *wrong* and we had to fight back, to end it. The Iniquitous needed to learn there were consequences to their actions and we would kill them for it.

It was funny, I'd never in a million years imagined myself becoming a killer, but this was my destiny. I knew that in my heart and soul. I could feel it like a vibrant thrum. I was a Chosen One, and I was chosen for *this*.

I could see it so easily now, my destiny wasn't clear, but I knew this was the path I was to follow.

What came after ... Well, I guessed I'd have to wait and see.

I heard the telltale soft patter of feet across the floor and a moment later Adelaide sat down beside me, curling her legs under her. Her dark hair was brushed out around her, taking up even more space than her small body.

"We can't stay here forever, can we?" she asked softly, her words flat—though with Adelaide they were almost always flat unless she was excited about something.

I shook my head. "No, we can't."

Both of us watched the view outside, the cars driving by on the street below completely oblivious to the secret apartment high above them—and frankly, to anything around them. It must be so easy to live in such a small bubble, one where the fantasy doesn't exist, and things are ... simple.

She exhaled a soft sigh beside me, but it was filled with worry.

"We'll be okay," I told her.

And we would be, okay as we could be, that was. I couldn't promise a miracle but I had to give her hope. Hope was our most valuable currency. Without hope we had nothing.

She slid her butt closer to me and laid her head on my shoulder.

"You know, you're like a sister to me," she confessed quietly. "I always wanted a sister."

I smiled too myself and rest my head against hers. "Me too."

Despite the heartbreak, the pain, and the confusion of the last year and a half, I wouldn't change a thing. I'd found the place where I belonged more than any other, and in the process learned it's not really a place, not at all, it's the people you surround yourself with who make you feel at home.

Of course there would always be things I missed of my human life, but this felt right in a way that before I hadn't realized I was even lacking anything. I hadn't known how much more I could have.

"What are you two whispering about?" Winston butted in, sitting down beside Adelaide.

"None of your business." She pushed his shoulder playfully and he pouted, pretending to be wounded. I smiled brightly. I loved watching the two of them together. They were as perfect as ...

As soon as my brain went in the direction of *Theodore* so did my eyes. I found him sitting across the room in a chair, a book clasped in his hands but his eyes ... his eyes were on me. I felt my lips part slightly as my breath was sucked out of me. How was it that he could do this to me with one single glance? That hardly seemed fair.

Sometimes I wished he could be a little less perfect, but then I would quickly realize even then he'd still be perfect to me.

Love, I'd come to realize, made you appreciate even the bad things about a person, their little ticks and quirks, because without them they wouldn't be the same person.

Jee walked into the room and stopped, surveying us all with narrowed eyes. "Well, don't you four look like the saddest, most mopiest bunch on the planet?"

"Is that even a word?" I countered.

He rolled his eyes. "Do I look like I care if it's a word or not?"

I shrugged. "Just thought I'd educate you in case you didn't." I smirked. Messing with Jee had quickly become one of my favorite pastimes.

He flipped me off and I let out a laugh I couldn't contain.

"Where's Ethan?" he asked. "I can't find him."

"Gym," Theo replied, not looking up from his book.

Jee huffed out a breath. "That explains why I couldn't find him. I avoid that place at all costs."

"Then why do you have one in your house?"

"For starters—I put it in for Ethan. Secondly, I actually enjoy it when a bunch of loud-mouthed Rugrats aren't in my house."

"Mhmm," I hummed doubtfully.

Jee was small, but he just had a naturally small body with little muscle. It was obvious he wasn't big on working out so he was a total liar.

My body had completely transformed, though. Where I'd once been soft and willowy I now felt more like a boulder. My legs were rock hard and I swore they entered a room before I did. My arms were toned and I could lift double my weight if I had to. Even my stomach was getting the telltale signs of potential abs. I wasn't sure how I felt about all of it yet but I damn sure was proud of myself. The difference in my body proved how hard I was working and it was paying off.

"Fine, don't believe me," he sighed dramatically in total Jee style.

He sauntered off down the hallway in the direction of the gym, putting even more swagger in his steps than usual.

"How on Earth you guys found him is beyond me," Theo muttered under his breath.

"Well, it was fairly easy you see since Ethan was banging him," Winston responded.

Theo lowered his book. His gray eyes narrowed into thin slits as he stared down the Brit.

"Thank you for the lovely visual I did not need. It was much appreciated."

"You're welcome," Winston said brightly.

Adelaide touched his arm and he looked over at her. "I think he was joking."

"Oh."

I shook my head. Some things seemed to go right over Winston's head. Theo's snide comments were usually one of them. I guessed being around Theo required you to ignore a lot of his commentary. Otherwise, the guy would actually be dead by now because someone would've strangled him.

Since my place by the window had been taken over by the two lovebirds, I moved to the couch. Being surrounded in such close quarters to everyone was wearing on me. There never seemed to be a moment to yourself. At least at the manor I'd had a private room, whereas here I didn't even have that luxury. It made thinking difficult and I was the type of person who needed space with my own thoughts to really think things through.

I was grateful for Jee taking us in and giving us a safe place to stay, but after this many months of it, I was tired.

Not to mention, everybody was nosy as all get out. If you frowned surely your whole world must be crumbling around you and you needed to talk about your emotions.

I knew my friends had been worried about me while we all believed Theo to be dead, but sometimes their concern went overboard and I felt smothered. There was already a lot of pressure on my shoulders and with them pressing me to talk about it and my *feelings* it could be too much.

Eventually, Adelaide and Winston's quiet giggling became too much for me and I got up. Knowing the gym was occupied by at least Ethan, but more than likely Jee had joined him too, I slid the elevator doors open and stepped inside then quietly closed them behind me. I might manage to get two minutes of peace and quiet in there, but I knew that was probably wishful thinking.

I didn't need to worry about anyone calling for the elevator since we were the only ones who used this one. Sliding down onto the floor I sat with my back against the wall of the elevator, leaned my head back, and closed my eyes.

Unsettled was the only way I could describe myself. I knew the feeling had to be contributing to my feelings of unrest and my need to be away from everyone.

The quiet of the elevator felt so strange, I'd been surrounded by constant chaos for so long, but it was much needed.

For the first time in a long time I felt clear, like I was breathing fresh mountain air and my eyes were wide open as I stood beneath the warm sun.

Eventually I drifted to sleep inside the elevator, the darkness behind my lids giving way to a dream and then a nightmare.

"So pretty," Thaddeus crowed, running his fingers through long dark hair.

I stood behind them, watching as he towered over the girl or the woman who I couldn't see.

A small whimper echoed in the dark room.

I looked around, trying to take stock of my surroundings. It seemed to be a basement— cinderblock walls, concrete walls—everything similar to most of my visions of Thaddeus.

"Youth," he crooned. "Wasted on the young. That's an oxymoron I believe, correct me if I'm wrong?"

Another whimper.

He tsked. "It's rude not to speak to your host. You are a guest in my house, are you not?"

She lifted her head. "I don't typically tie up my guests," she spat.

Her voice.

No.

It couldn't be.

"Oh, Danielle." He touched her cheek. *"I'm thoroughly going to enjoy killing you."*

With a scream, I came awake. Then I screamed again, panicked at my unfamiliar surroundings.

In seconds, the doors were thrust open and I was pulled into Theo's arms.

"Mara? What is it?"

I grabbed onto his shoulders and buried my head into his neck, sobbing.

"Mara? Talk to me, please," he begged, stroking my hair and trying to comfort me.

I could barely breathe I was freaking out so much.

My worst nightmare had come true. I'd thought I'd done everything right, but Thaddeus was always one step ahead of us. Always. We would never beat him, how could we when he was so cunning?

"He has her," I choked out. "He has Dani."

"Dani?" Theo pulled me back looking into my eyes with concern.

"Dani," I repeated. *"Dani."*

Finally, a look of understanding crossed his features. "Your friend."

"Yes," I cried. "He's going to kill her. Theo, we can't stay here and do nothing, we can't. We have to try to save her, and if we can't we still have to do *something*. He has to be stopped."

He looked over his shoulder and it was then I noticed the others gathered behind him. I'm sure they'd come running when he did but I'd only been aware of his presence. It overshadowed everything else.

Theo looked at them and they must've agreed because he looked back at me, steel in his eyes.

"Okay." He nodded to his own word. "Okay, we'll go."

chapter twenty-six

In RECORD TIME WE PACKED everything and by everything I mean all the things we showed up with months ago, plus bags upon bags of weapons. Even Nigel was scooped up in Theo's arms. At least he wasn't arguing with me about leaving the cat this time. I think we all knew we wouldn't be coming back here. As the five us piled in the elevator Jee stood, looking back in fondness at his apartment before stepping on and closing the doors.

"I thought you were staying here," Ethan breathed in shock.

Jee shrugged. "I couldn't watch you leave me this time. Not when ..."

Not when you might not come back, was what he left unsaid.

Ethan kissed him and whispered something in his ear.

I looked around at the five people gathered. People who had become like family to me and I wondered if it was possible for us to storm wherever it was Thaddeus was hiding out and for all of us to escape unscathed.

The odds didn't seem likely.

Six people against an army of Iniquitous.

Yeah, we were screwed.

This was stupid, but we had to try. Dani didn't deserve to die by Thaddeus's hands. He had to be stopped and no one else was going to do it.

We were the only ones stupid enough to try. It was funny how stupidity and bravery went hand in hand. You couldn't have one without the other.

As the elevator went down, Theo reached for my hand and gave it a small squeeze before releasing it. He knew I was scared, and definitely worried, but he also knew just as I did that we had to do this.

The doors opened and we loaded everything into Jee's two cars. Ethan and Jee decided to take the Corvette, which left the four of us with the Range Rover. Theo, of course, insisted on driving.

Shocker.

I took the passenger seat with Adelaide and Winston in the back. They were quiet, all of us lost in our thoughts. Maybe we were all afraid if one of us spoke then we'd chicken out or something. Theo handed me Nigel and he curled up into my lap and fell asleep in seconds, purring softly.

Theo pulled out onto the street with the others following in the other car since Theo was the only one who knew where we were going. None of us had asked him where Thaddeus was and I doubt he would've told us, even me, if we had.

"How long of a drive is it?" I asked softly, my voice barely above a whisper.

"Not long enough," he replied cryptically.

I turned to the window watching as rain sluiced against it. The sky was a deep gray, nearly black in places despite the fact it was the afternoon. It seemed to reflect our melancholy back on us like some strange foggy mirror.

My heart ached for my human friend. The one I felt I'd abandoned because I had to. I'd believed I was doing the right thing, but apparently I couldn't have been more wrong. He was still trying to use her against me.

I wiped away a tear that had escaped and was slowly making its way down my cheek.

I hated feeling so helpless.

Nothing was in my control, but I guess it was a joke to think I had any chance at control at all.

Maybe that was my fatal flaw—wanting to have all the answers, to be the puppeteer of my own life, my own destiny. I hated to think I had no choice in the matter, that everything was already plotted out by someone or something else and I had to let it play out.

It's okay to cry. It doesn't make you weak.

I startled at the sound of Theo's voice echoing through my mind. He hadn't spoken to me in this way since he'd been back.

It's not for that reason that I don't want to cry. I feel like if I cry it means he wins. I don't want him to have any kind of power over me.

Thaddeus has no power over you, Mara. He never has and he never will. He's weak. Power doesn't always equal strength.

I can't believe he's my dad. I don't want him to be. I don't want any part of him to be a part of me.

Oh, Mara. You are nothing like him. Blood is nothing.

I want to believe you.

You should.

I quiet my mind to him. I don't want him to know but my biggest fear is becoming like Thaddeus.

He was like me, a Chosen One, and somehow, he turned into what he's become. If it happened to him, what's to say it couldn't happen to me?

***

As the sky darkened into night I could tell Theo grew tenser and tenser. His shoulders were tight and his grip on the wheel was white knuckled. Even his jaw was clenched in a steel vice. I knew there was nothing I could say to comfort him, not when the night was when we were most vulnerable to the Iniquitous and when we were heading back to the place where he'd been tortured for months. Even though Theo claimed he could've left at any time and he was gathering information I wasn't sure I believed him completely. There was more he wasn't telling and I feared he might *never* be ready to talk about it. It broke my heart he'd been in the clutches of Thaddeus. The man was pure evil.

And now it's Dani in his clutches.

At least Theo was an enchanter, a protector at that so he had even more powers at his disposal, but not Dani. She was only a human, and to someone like Thaddeus he could squash her like a bug and not even realize what he'd done until it was too late.

I glanced in the backseat and found the other two sleeping. Adelaide had her head pillowed on Winston's shoulder while Winston rested his against the window. Behind us the headlights of the Corvette shined brightly as Ethan and Jee followed us.

"Will we be stopping tonight?" I asked Theo.

He shook his head. "No. It's safer to keep moving."

"Do you want me to drive some? You've already been driving a few hours."

Again, he shook his head. "I'd rather drive."

I knew what he wasn't saying—he'd rather be in control of the situation.

"You should get your rest," he told me softly, his eyes never straying from the road.

"I'm not sleepy," I lied.

The car was lulling me to sleep with the steady *swish swish swish* of the wipers, but I didn't want to leave Theo without company. If he wanted to talk I wanted to be awake to listen.

He glanced over at me and gave me a small smile. "Seriously, Mara. I'm fine. Get some rest, you're going to need it."

I knew he was right, but still I resisted.

Soon, though, it became too much and sleep overtook me.

***

I awoke a few hours later. It was still pitch black outside and our surroundings were completely unfamiliar. "Where are we?" I asked sleepily, looking around at the entirely flat land with nothing to see for miles. Long gone were the bustling city streets.

"Ohio," Theo answered.

I studied his profile and while he looked weary he also looked determined.

"Thaddeus is hiding out in Ohio?" I remarked dryly.

Of all the places I thought we'd find Thaddeus and his cronies, Ohio was not one of them.

He nodded. "Yeah, shocking I know."

"Do you know why Ohio?"

He shrugged, his eyes steadfastly on the road. "I'm not sure. Maybe he grew up here or maybe it was convenient. Whatever the reason I'm sure it's not profound."

In the back the other two were still sleeping and I knew I should try to get some more rest, but I wasn't sleepy anymore.

"When are we stopping?" I asked, looking at the clock. The sun would be rising in less than two hours.

"Soon," he replied. "We'll stop at a hotel and get some rest."

"Is that safe?" I inquired softly.

He didn't answer.

***

Theo slept soundly in the queen-sized bed with Nigel curled on the pillow beside him while I sat in the chair by the window. The other bed was occupied by a sleeping Ethan and Jee while Adelaide and Winston went to pick up food from the hotel restaurant. Theo had made Winston vow with his life to protect Adelaide if anything happened.

I felt nervous, my body vibrating with a restless energy. Out there somewhere nearby Dani might be dead or she might be fighting for her life. I hated feeling stuck here, but I knew the others needed to sleep before we did anything, and even once we did act it might be too late or...

Or it could be pointless.

At the end of the day we were practically kids.

The door squeaked open and Adelaide tiptoed in first with food. The three of us sat on the floor eating as quietly as possible to not disturb the others. They'd picked up cheeseburgers and fries, and I wasn't sure if it was actually amazing or I was just starving but I was certain it was the best thing I'd ever eaten. It was probably a weird time to be eating a cheeseburger, but we needed more than eggs and toast.

A few hours later the others woke up and ate, then it was time to leave.

Once again we found ourselves piling into the car.

This time my heart raced a mile a minute, knowing each second brought us nearer to Thaddeus. I was afraid, I wouldn't lie or pretend I wasn't scared, but I wasn't backing down, either. This had to be done, not only for Dani, but for Theo who I'd believed had been killed, for all the other innocents he'd murdered in cold blood, and ... and for my mother. The woman I never got to know because he took her away from me. My father too, the only man I'd ever known as a father, who I'd never see again and all he'd ever done was try to keep me safe. Thaddeus was sadistic. He got off on killing others for no good reason. He might've been Iniquitous, but he was also a plain cold-blooded killer.

Adelaide and Winston were subdued in the back, and Theo was stone-faced beside me. None of us seemed to want to speak. Eventually, Theo pulled down a gravel road and parked.

"We walk from here," he announced, shutting off the engine and stuffing the keys in his pocket.

We filed out of the car and loaded up with weapons.

Nigel meowed from the backseat.

"Sorry, man, but you have to stay here," Theo told him. He'd made sure to leave all the windows down halfway so he could get air, or get out if he had to, but since it was cool out we didn't have to worry about him getting too hot.

I loaded weapons onto my pants, thankful for the built in straps on the leather pants. Jee looked over at me and chuckled. "Let's hope you're as badass as you look."

I stuck my tongue out at him, which wasn't very badass of me, but whatever.

Once we were all loaded up with weapons we began the trek through the woods. Theo led the way with the rest of us trailing behind.

We all walked as silently as we could, afraid if we made any single small little noise someone might jump out from behind a tree and get us.

After several miles the trees began to thin and opened up into a valley below with one of the largest houses I'd ever seen. It was very clearly a mansion, with two levels above ground spreading far and wide. I'd never seen a home so wide before, not even the manor. The six of us stood side-by-side staring down at the home. If you didn't know the evil living behind those walls you'd think it was the beautiful home of someone famous. The lawn was immaculate and there were even flowers planted around the house. I was surprised there wasn't a fence or gate of some sort, but I guessed when you were the king of all evil and lived in the middle of nowhere you weren't too concerned about people finding you or being bold enough to attack.

I couldn't decide if we were crazy or stupid, but it was probably a mix of both.

"We'll go around the side," Theo directed. "I know a spot to get in. They patrol the outside at night, but during the day they can't. They have humans working for them," he admitted with a bite of his lip. "They're terrified, so don't harm them, just knock them out so they can't raise the alarm."

"Humans? Why?" I asked.

Theo looked at me and heaved out a heavy sigh. "He views humans as beneath all paranormal creatures. They're slaves to him."

I felt like gagging. "He needs to be stopped," I growled, anger bubbling inside me. I couldn't believe I shared DNA with this being. I scrubbed at my arms like I could scrub what parts of me were Thaddeus from my body.

Theo grabbed my hands and held them in his so I'd stop.

Looking into my eyes he said, "You're nothing like him, Mara. *Nothing*. Never forget that."

I crashed my lips to his and he kissed me back.

I rested my forehead against his. "I love you."

"Don't you say goodbye to me," he warned, steel in his voice.

I cracked a small smile. "It's not goodbye if it's true."

He kissed me again. "This is not the end, Mara."

"I know."

I didn't know, but it felt better to say it.

Jee faked a yawn. "All these endearments are cute and all, but don't we have a bad guy to kill and a damsel in distress to save?"

His sarcasm managed to break the bubble of seriousness that had formed around us.

"It's time," Theo said, reaching for my hand.

Then we began the descent down to the mansion.

chapter twenty-seven

W E CIRCLED AROUND THE SIDE and slowly made our way to a window low on the back of the house. Theo held up a finger, shushing us even though we hadn't made a peep, and with a swish of his fingers the window began to rise.

Ethan went in first followed by Jee, Winston, Adelaide, then me, with Theo coming in last.

The room we'd entered seemed to be some sort of storage cellar. There were rows of black plastic shelves lined with food items and other household things like shampoos and conditioners. I guessed even the Iniquitous had to wash their hair.

"What are they? Extreme couponers or hoarders here?" Jee asked in a disgusted tone. "Both are scary."

"Scarier than being Iniquitous?" I raised a brow.

He shrugged. "Well, there's that too."

"Can you two be quiet?" Theo hissed, glaring at us.

Jee rolled his eyes and I mimed zipping my lips.

Theo crooked a finger, silently ordering us to follow him. We stepped into a hallway lined with doors on either side and sconces on the wall.

"This is trippy," Jee said. "Why are there so many hallways?"

It was then I noticed there seemed to be branches in every direction with more doors and even more hallways.

"How will we find our way out?" I whispered to Theo.

"I'll know the way."

We walked straight down the hallway we were on before turning right down another.

Theo seemed to know where he was taking us but I didn't know how. Jee was right, this was trippy; it was set up like a maze and I couldn't help but wonder if it was done on purpose in case someone tried to escape.

Theo stopped suddenly and held up his hand for us to do the same.

He seemed to be thinking.

A piercing scream echoed from up ahead.

"Dani!" I screamed back, taking off.

"Mara, no!" Theo shouted behind me as I ran.

I didn't stop, though.

She screamed again and I knew I was getting closer.

The others' feet pounded after me, begging me to stop, but I didn't listen. He was torturing Dani, maybe even killing her in this very moment. We didn't have a second to spare.

Another scream and I turned to my right. There was only one door here and I ran forward, pushing it open.

It slammed closed behind me and I turned to look over my shoulder, watching as it glimmered like someone had tossed glitter at it. But I knew it wasn't glitter.

Force field maybe? Some spell of some sort, I was certain.

The door banged behind me as I'm sure Theo and the others tried to get in but couldn't.

I turned back around and found Dani slumped in a chair. Just like in my vision her back was to me. I wasn't sure if she was still breathing or not so I stepped forward to check. I barely made it two steps before I felt like a hand was crushing my windpipe.

"You move when I say you can move." The voice came from the corner of the room and I turned my head a miniscule amount, it was all I could muster, and found Thaddeus in the corner crouched down. He looked tired, haggard. His eyes boasted dark circles but the manic look still remained. His hair was tousled, not like he'd been running his fingers through it but as if it had been electrified. There was something off about him, I mean there'd always been, but this was more. This was

... This was a man losing his mind and he didn't even know it.

"My daughter, we finally meet in person." His voice crackled like flames.

He stood and walked toward me. He didn't look as healthy as he did in my visions and I wondered if he had intended me to see everything and purposely masked himself. His skin was a pale white, almost gray, if I didn't know better I might think he was a vampire. At the very least it was obvious he hadn't seen the sun in a long time but being Iniquitous he'd most likely be sleeping during the day anyway since his powers were strongest at night. He certainly wasn't sleeping now, though, and he looked as if he hadn't slept in weeks.

"I thought for sure you'd come to me when I spoke of a brother you had. Surely poor orphaned Mara would be so curious about a sibling she'd never heard of that she'd have to come to have her questions answered. But maybe you saw through my lie."

"Lie?" I choked out and he lessened the pressure on my neck. It was still there, spreading to my entire body so I felt as if I was trapped prisoner.

He grinned. "So you believed me then?" He laughed gleefully. "You have no brother, Mara. No mother, and the man you thought was your father? Well, I killed him too. The only family you have left, the only blood you share, is with me." As he spoke his face grew nearer and nearer to the side of mine. If I could've shivered I would have when he touched the inside of my arm. His skin felt like ice and thin like paper.

"Well, as you see, I knew I had to do *more* to get you here. Something big. And that's where this beautiful young lady came into play. Punished for the sole reason of knowing my daughter."

"Don't call me that," I spat.

He clucked his tongue and grabbed my face in one hand squeezing until I flinched.

"You. Are. My. Daughter. My blood runs through these veins and I need it."

"Why do you need it?"

"Look at me, I am growing weak. My power, while strong, drains my life force. But you … you are young, and as my daughter you can sustain me."

I tried to shake out of his grasp but couldn't. If I could've cried I would have. I felt dirty where he touched me, like what he was could corrode my skin and poison me.

"Is she alive?" I asked, unable to look at Dani's slumped form.

"For now," he answered cryptically, "but if you don't cooperate that could change."

He released me and stepped back. The spell he'd cast over me lifted and feeling began to return to my limbs. I rubbed my hands together trying to shake away the tingling of the nerves.

There was more banging on the door behind us. "Your friends are quite determined. I admire their spunk. It's too bad they'll have to die."

"Don't you dare touch them," I bit out. "I'll do whatever you ask if you let them go."

He shrugged. "You'll do whatever I ask regardless. Mara, you're not the one bargaining here. I'm in charge. There is so outcome here where you win and I lose. It doesn't work like that."

He moved to a seat in the corner. A large leather armchair that was so at odds to the rickety chair Dani was strapped to.

"Sit," he ordered.

Before I could ask where, he swished his hand, sparks tingling at the tips, and a chair similar to his appeared out of nowhere.

I sat before he could order me again or force me to do it. I figured maybe if I cooperated he'd be less prickly.

"So why all the lies?" I asked, leaning forward in the chair. "Why not tell me what you needed?"

"Would you have come?"

I swallowed and stayed silent. We both already knew what the answer was.

I cleared my throat awkwardly. I couldn't believe I was having a conversation with Thaddeus, my *father*—I nearly gagged at the words—while my friends wondered what had happened to me and Dani lay hurt. But I needed to keep him talking. If he was talking then he wasn't hurting anyone. "Are you dying?"

He waved his hand dismissively. "What a silly question. We are all *dying*, Mara. Every second of every day we all grow closer to our demise. For some of us that time comes sooner than others, but what we all have in common is we never know *when*. That's what scares us, the unknown of it all. We don't know when it'll happen or what'll come after."

"Are you afraid to die?"

"I am not, because I won't die. Not once I get your blood. But you ..." He sat back in the chair, crossed his legs, and laced his fingers together. "I hope the afterlife treats you well, my dear."

"I'm sure it'll be better than how you've treated me," I said with more spark than I felt. His words had shaken me but I couldn't let him know. He ate off of fear, thrived on it, and I would not contribute to something that made him so gleeful.

He chuckled like my words amused him. Everything seemed to.

"You're not dead yet, are you, my child? I'd say I've treated you much better than many of my other ... *guests*. And you're not even my guest, you came here uninvited."

"You wanted me to come here," I reminded him.

He grinned. "The logistics do not matter here. You still broke into *my* home."

"And your people raided the manor. You killed innocent people."

"I can not be held responsible for what my followers do. As long as they follow my orders they're free to enjoy themselves." He grinned maliciously. "If they don't follow my orders then they know better than to return.

The consequences are dire." His smiled faded and his brows knit together. "After they let you escape from the manor there were many of my most valued ... companions I had to unfortunately dispose of."

"I would apologize but I'm not sorry."

He smiled and it was actually a genuinely amused smile.

"No, I suppose you aren't." He stared at me for a moment and then whispered, "You look exactly like her."

"Why'd you kill her?" I asked. "If you loved her, why'd you do it?"

It's a question that'd been haunting me. I cannot imagine killing the one I loved. The thought of bringing harm to Theo made me feel sick to my stomach.

He looked away, his eyes growing foggy, and I knew he was lost in a time long ago.

Slowly, his gaze drifted back to me. "It's what I was chosen to do."

chapter twenty-eight

WHATEVER I'D BEEN EXPECTING HIM to say, it wasn't that.

I sat, shocked, trying to process his words.

It's what I was chosen to do.

Just as much as I knew I'd been chosen to kill him, to eradicate the Iniquitous, his had been to kill my mom.

But *why?*

She'd been *good* and kind and ... I might not have known her but I knew she had to be extraordinary.

"Why?" I voiced.

"Why does anything happen, Mara?" he asked. "Why does the sun rise and the wolf howl? Sometimes, the dots connect and while we don't like the picture the outcome is unavoidable."

"But you had to *kill* her? How could you possibly be chosen to do that? It seems like a weak ass pitiful excuse to me—"

I choked as air was cut off at my throat. He hadn't moved but it felt as if fingers were digging into my throat. I could even feel the indentation of his fingertips.

"Do you think I *wanted* this? *Any* of this? We don't choose our destinies, Mara; our destinies choose us."

The pressure let up. "I refuse to believe that," I told him vehemently, but it came out as a gasping whisper.

"Then you're nothing but a naïve child," he crowed.

I rubbed my throat, tears piercing my eyes but I refused to let them fall.

"It's time you grew up, Mara," he snapped. "This is the real world you're in now. People *die* for reasons we don't understand and sometimes we're the ones that have to kill them."

I knew I should have kept my mouth shut but, of course, I didn't. "It sounds to me like you're trying to make excuses to make yourself feel better."

Power slammed into me and I flew out of the chair and across the room. My whole body hit the cinderblock wall and pain radiated through my body. My skull cracked against it and I fell to the floor in a heap as everything faded to nothing.

***

When I came to it was dark and I couldn't be sure if it was only hours that had passed or more than a day. Upon looking around I surmised that Thaddeus was gone. My body ached with stiffness not just from hitting the wall, but the way I'd been scrunched on the floor.

I picked my body up off the floor slowly. Nothing seemed to be broken but the back of my head throbbed as if it had its own heartbeat.

I let out a groan and crept over to where Dani was slouched in the chair. I pressed my fingers to her neck searching for a pulse. I held my own breath and began to grow panicky when I couldn't find it.

Keep your cool, Mara.

Then I found it. It was faint, barely a flutter, but it was there and it meant she was alive.

Exhausted, I sat down beside her, resting my head against her leg. She wasn't conscious but I felt by being close to her she'd sense my presence and know she was safe and I was going to get her out of there.

I wondered where Theo and the others had gone, if Thaddeus had rounded them up or they'd gotten out and were coming back for me. I knew I couldn't rely on them, though. As much as I loved and trusted them I knew I had to depend on myself.

I needed to rest. My body had been through a rampage. It felt as if I'd been squashed by a rhinoceros. I closed my eyes, not planning to fall asleep, but somehow I did.

***

This time when I woke it was still dark out, a sliver of moonlight shining into the barren room, and Thaddeus was back. He sat in his chair. His hands crossed in front of his face watching me.

I jolted away from Dani as if I'd been caught doing something I shouldn't have.

He continued to stare at me, not saying a word. I felt icky being looked at by him, as if his evil was a tangible thing that could reach me across the room. I guessed it was, if he wanted it to. I swallowed thickly, trying not to show fear but it was impossible. I *was* afraid of him. I would be stupid not to be. But just because I was afraid didn't mean I couldn't or wouldn't fight back.

"You know, I didn't know about you for the longest time," he mused quietly, almost reverently. "Your mother, for whatever reason, kept you a secret from me. I suppose maybe she was already scared of me at that point and wanted to hide you away. I would've never harmed you, though. Not my child, my daughter, my heir. I would've kept you safe, protected."

"But you killed her?" I interrupted.

"Because I had to," he growled. "You, young one, have not learned how tied to our destinies we are. How they become you and eat away at you until you fulfill them. I turned to the Iniquitous, seeking power that would prevent my destiny from coming true, little did I know I'd taken the first step in fulfilling it. *We have no choice*," he reiterated.

I began to shake all over from cold and realized his anger was making the room absolutely frigid.

"You think choices you make are yours but they're not. Nothing is ours. Fate fucks us all."

I held onto the leg of Dani's chair. I could feel bile rising in the back of my throat. The last thing I wanted, or needed, was to get sick and throw up all over the floor.

He got up from the chair and squatted down in front of me.

"I tried to kill myself, once I realized I was going to have to kill her." I noticed he'd never said her name, maybe it was too painful for him. Maybe he really did regret everything. "Look." He ripped his shirt open, revealing a nasty looking scar, like someone had taken a sword and drove it into his body and down, ripping it open to spill out his insides. "I did this to myself. No one should've survived this. I thought I didn't until I woke up, my chest having knitted itself back together and leaving behind a raging red scar. We don't die until it's our time, Mara. They tell you it's because you're special." He leaned in close so close I held my breath as his lips touched my ear. "But it's because we're cursed."

I shivered as he backed away, his words reverberating through my skull.

We're cursed.

Was he right? I didn't want to believe him, I wanted to think only lies ever spewed from his lips, but the haunted look in his eyes was all too real.

"Where are my friends?" I asked him, trying to change the subject before I went down the rabbit hole with it.

He shrugged, settling into his chair once more. "I do not know. They are not here. It seems you are not as important to them as they are to you." He smiled evilly then, pleased at having something like this to hold against me.

I didn't let his words bother me. I trusted my friends. They wouldn't leave me unless they either had to or were getting help.

He stood then. "I'll be back later. My guard will bring you food and water. Try not to bite him."

In a puff of smoke he was gone.

I rolled my eyes. "Dramatic much?"

But it was a neat trick.

While I was alone I tended to Dani, ripping up my clothes and wrapping her wounds as best I could. She groaned but never regained consciousness. I spoke to her, telling her she'd be okay and I was going to get her out of here. I didn't know if she could hear me, but it made me feel better to think she could. It broke my heart to see her suffering like this all because of knowing me.

Maybe Thaddeus was right. We were cursed. And we cursed everyone around us just by knowing us.

chapter twenty-nine

AS PROMISED, FOOD WAS BROUGHT to me. The man who brought it made sure to kick me in the ribs before he left. I didn't retaliate as much as I wanted to, because I knew my punishment would be much worse than some bruised ribs.

The meal was surprisingly delicious, not the scraps I'd expected, and I ate it quickly. In hindsight, I shouldn't have since it could've been laced with something, but I was too hungry to think straight.

I finished eating and shoved the plate away. He'd given me water too and I sipped some before tipping some down Dani's throat. Her tongue came to life lapping slowly at the drops of water.

"Oh, Dani. I'm so sorry." I smoothed her hair away from her forehead and a tear leaked from my eye onto her forehead. "This is all my fault."

I wasn't sure if I would ever be able to forgive myself for the pain I'd brought everyone who knew me. I was a plague, bringing death wherever I went.

I gave her a little more water before sitting back down on the floor beside her.

Was what Thaddeus said true? Had he had no choice but to kill my mom? I always thought it was because she ran away with me and he wanted to retaliate, but what if that wasn't it at all? What if all of this had been set in motion long ago by something beyond any of our control?

Suddenly, nothing seemed to make sense.

More hours passed, I slept, I woke up, and even more time passed before Thaddeus made his return.

The foggy black smoke seeped from the ceiling and solidified into his shape.

"It's time," he declared cryptically.

"Time for what?"

He flew at me and I found myself pressed against the wall. A knife was held to my throat and my eyes widened with fear.

Theo! I shouted into my mind. *Theo, I'm so sorry. I love you.*

Thaddeus licked his lips gleefully and pinned my left arm above my head.

I focused on my center, trying to find my magic to shove him off of me, but there was nothing. Not a flicker. Not anything. It was as dried up as the Sahara desert and I didn't understand it.

"You're magic doesn't work here, light one," he growled, plunging the knife into my arm.

I screamed as he dragged it down, tearing open my flesh. Blood pumped freely from my arm, dripping down my flesh and onto the floor.

He let me go and I dropped to the floor like a rag doll. I clutched my arm, trying to stop the bleeding but there was so much. In the little jar around my neck the firefly buzzed madly.

With a manic smile Thaddeus pulled a vial of a smoking deep purple potion from his pocket and uncorked it. He tipped the knife, letting my blood spill into it. When that wasn't enough he grabbed me up by injured arm, causing me to scream in pain, and bled me into the vial. The color of the potion changed from eggplant to a deep emerald and he swirled it around.

Dropping me once more he backed away and with a pleased laugh he drank the potion.

I held my arm tightly, trying to stop the bleeding, but scarlet still dripped around my pale fingers.

I love you, I love you, I love you. I thought over and over again. I didn't know if he could hear me, but I assumed he could, and I wanted him to know when I died my last thought would be of him.

I glanced over at Dani, saying more silent apologies because I couldn't get her out of here. I couldn't save her.

Thaddeus began to choke and I looked over at him, finding the veins in all his body turning black. His face looked grotesque like some kind of monster with all the roads of black on his face.

"No," he growled, looking at his hands. "No, it's not possible."

He ran at me and grabbed me by the throat.

"What have you done to me?" He shook me.

I couldn't answer him.

He shook me some before dropping me. I let out a grunt.

"It's not possible," he repeated. He bent down at me, staring right at me with his head tilted. The black was spreading to the capillaries in his eyes. He pushed my head back and tilted my chin. Appraising me from every angle.

"I was blinded before, blinded by your mother's beauty in you so I couldn't see it."

"Couldn't see what?" I bit out gravelly, my throat raw and my body screaming in pain as my life force drained from me.

"That you are not my daughter. You're *his*."

I had no time to react to his words, because there was a large explosion, massive really since it shook the whole place, even this stone underground part.

"No." With one word he disappeared into his puff of smoke and was gone.

There was another explosion and I knew this was my chance to escape. I was barely in any shape to get myself out, let alone an unconscious person, but I couldn't leave Dani here.

With my good hand I slapped her hard, I hated to do it but I needed to rouse her enough that she could support some of her weight.

I tugged and kicked at the door trying to get open.

Once more, I tried my magic and this time it worked. The door blew apart into a million little pieces. Whatever spell had been cast on the room was broken now.

I went back for Dani, tossing her arm over my shoulder and dragging her from the room.

My vision was growing blurry and I wasn't sure I could even remember how to get back to the room we'd come into the mansion in, but I had to try, even if I died doing it.

Dani's head lolled to the side and she threw up. Her body grew slack against me.

"Come on, Dani. I need you to help me out here," I begged.

I pulled her further down the hall while I leaned against one of the walls for my own support. My body was so tired and weak and my arm was still bleeding.

I turned to my left, hoping I made the right choice.

Another explosion rocked the building and I lost my balance, dropping Dani and falling to the ground myself.

I began to cry from the pain, but I refused to give up. I was not dying without a fight.

I somehow managed to get Dani up again and wrapped my arm around her waist.

"We can do this," I said more for myself than her.

I began to smell smoke and I knew a fire had been started. There were screams above us and running feet. This was our chance for escape.

I gritted my teeth and did my best to forget the pain.

Another explosion at the end of the hall sent us flying through the air.

My body felt more broken and battered than it had before. I tried to get up, to move, to do something, but I couldn't. I could barely see my vision was so foggy at this point. Ash and sparks of flame floated in front of me. It was really kind of pretty. I guessed this was a better way to die than being beaten to death by Thaddeus.

A dark shadow fell over me and I couldn't see the person's face. I knew it was male from the shape of the broad shoulders but I didn't think it was Theo. I didn't get that familiar buzz I got when he was near. I didn't even know if the person was friend or foe, but I begged, "Save her. Save her please. She doesn't deserve to die."

The person said nothing. He just bent and scooped me into his arms like a rag doll. My head lolled back. I had no fight left in me.

Around me the mansion began to burn. I knew it had to be some sort of enchanted fire to burn the cinderblock that encased us.

Through my foggy eyes I saw the brightness of daylight, freedom I hoped, and I swore I saw the shapes of my friends. I smiled to myself, whispering "Theo," and then my eyes closed for the final time.

Possess, the final book in *The Enchanted* series, coming soon.

acknowledgements

This book is so long coming, and I want to thank my readers for being so patient with me. I didn't want to force this book and I needed to let it simmer for a while, so thank you for allowing me to do that. I'm happy that so many of you fell in love with Enchant and couldn't wait for more. The best is yet to come I promise. I can't wait to get Possess into your hands.

A big thank you to Wendi the best editor and formatter ever for putting up with me this last year and my crazy schedule since my health dictated my life. I love you so much girl and I don't know what I did before you. I mean that. Thanks for cracking the whip.

Thank you to Regina Wamba and Yuli Xenexai for the incredible photo shoot for this series and the amazing covers. They're so beautiful and I couldn't love them more.

Thank you to my family and all my writer friends for constantly motivating me to keep going. Love y'all!

Thank you to everyone who's read Enchant, and now this book, and is hopefully eager for Possess. It's been so fun to venture back into paranormal. I've missed it a lot.

Until the next time...

XOXO,

Micalea

38557127R00175

Made in the USA
Middletown, DE
09 March 2019